Semi-Broken

Isabel Jordan

ISBN-10: 1979302227
ISBN-13: 978-1979302227

Praise for *Semi-Charmed*

"*Harper is a heroine you can get behind! She's witty, crazy, kick-ass, and amazing! Noah is my new book boyfriend! He's the bad boy we all want and your mom hates but then she falls in love with him, too!*"

—Indy Book Fairy

"*Fresh and fun. Relaxed with a good dose of humor.*"

—Lanie's Book Thoughts

"*Semi-Charmed is well paced, fun and easy to read.*"

—TJ Loves to Read

"*The hero and heroine were intriguing and engaging.*"

—Smexy Books

"*Holy crap! That was awesome! More please!! Brilliantly funny, sexy, charming, and awesome.*" —

Me, Myself & Books

"*If you are a fan of the Sookie Stackhouse books, Buffy the Vampire slayer, and the likes, you will enjoy this book a great deal.*"

—The Book Disciple

Praise for *Semi-Human*

"A fun and sexy, sweet and exciting story about a smart, witty and kick-ass heroine, a swoony, intense and equally badass hero." --TJ Loves to Read

"Harper Hall is the best kind of heroine for me. She's funny, snarky, can handle herself in a fight and never shies away from telling anyone what she's thinking. Long-story-short, this series is worth a read. Just don't read it in public because there are parts that are snort-laugh inducing (and no one looks hot while snort-laughing)." --Knockin' Books

"As for Riddick, well that dude just has issues. I'm just gonna say it, he's that really hot guy, ya know the one who's crazy that you should inch away from, but instead you give your number. Yep, that one." --Lanie's Book Thoughts

"The snark, the humor, the sarcasm, the love. This is a well-rounded, well-written novel and an awesome progression for the series." --Me, Myself & Books

"I went into this book hoping to get the same feelings I got from the last book. I was not disappointed. This book was great from beginning to end. The characters I loved in the last book were there for me again." --Pixies Can Read Blogspot

Praise for *Semi-Twisted*

"Isabel Jordan delivers a laugh out loud, action packed, entertaining read with sassy dialogues and pop culture references that made me smile like a loon." --TJ Loves to Read

"All in all, as with other books in the series, this one is perfect for fans of the PNR genre, and for fans of adult contemporary romance with lots of humor and just a hint of edge. It's definitely one for the keeper shelves!" --Knockin' Books

"If you love Charley Davison, True Blood or Buffy the Vampire Slayer, then you will definitely want to read this quirky vampire/paranormal series." –Literati Literature Lovers

"I waited FOREVER for this book…at least it seemed that way. I couldn't wait to read Mischa and Hunter's story! True to the author's form, I giggled my way through this story, when I wasn't sighing over the leading man." –Author L.E. Wilson

DEDICATION

To Connor, my lead engineer. The dog poop cannon is a great idea and I definitely want one. But can you finish plans for my Death Star first? Thanks.

ACKNOWLEDGMENTS

First of all, thanks to my husband Don for giving me the freedom (and the office space) to follow my dreams. (And I swear to God, I love you, but if you ask me “is it done” one more time, I won’t be held responsible for my actions.)

Thanks to Connor for helping me keep my sarcasm skills sharp. You’re learning quickly, and one day, my son, the pupil will out snark the master.

Thanks to my parents who have never failed to support me in all my efforts. I wouldn’t be doing any of this without you.

Thanks to L.E. Wilson for your support, advice, and superior BETA reading skills. Without you, everyone would be left to wonder who the hell was taking care of the baby.

Thanks to Renee Wright for your keen editing eye (and for your tolerance of my many, many typos), and to The Design Dude at Knockin’ Books for my fan-freakin’-tastic cover art.

Big thanks to Tania Gray for providing consistent writing motivation (often in the most hilarious ways possible). You helped me stay focused on what was really important (i.e.: getting the damn book done).

And last but far from least, huge thanks to all the fabulous readers who've stayed with me on this crazy journey. The fact that you guys not only *get* my weird sense of humor but *enjoy* it shocks the hell out of me and makes me the happiest (and luckiest) writer in the world. I've said it before and it's still totally inadequate, but thanks. You all mean the world to me.

CHAPTER ONE

Watching the woman he loved marry someone else could make a man do some pretty crazy shit. And watching her have a baby with the monosyllabic douchebag?

Well, now *that* could make a man do some *semi-suicidal* shit.

Lucas Cooper was walking, talking, breathing proof of that fact at the moment.

He could almost see the headlines now: *Former Vampire Crimes Unit police detective arrested for impersonating a doctor and kidnapping a mental patient.*

Awesome. His mom would be so fucking proud.

Lucas ran a finger under the starched collar of his stolen lab coat and frowned at the girl through the tiny barred window on the triple-chained cell door. "Are you sure that's her?"

To his left, Dr. Violet Marchand pulled the girl's medical chart out of the plastic sleeve on the door. Flipping through the first few pages, she said, "That's her. Not what you expected?"

Hell no, Lucas thought. Hospital security had described her as a brutal killer. He'd been expecting to see someone larger, more imposing, dangerous-looking. Less…delicate and feminine. "How long has she been in solitary?"

"Since her last escape attempt."

Lucas glanced at her, incredulous. "That was over six years ago. She's been in this cell ever since?"

Violet shoved her glasses up with her index finger. "Yes. She's actually very lucky. When supernatural patients don't respond to treatment, they're usually…eliminated."

Lucas wasn't so sure that anyone stuck in this place could ever be called *lucky*.

The psych ward at Midvale Prison was pretty much upstate New York's version of Arkham Asylum. It was dark, it was scary, and it reeked of foulness Lucas didn't even want to contemplate. Human patients would never be expected to live in such conditions. But the only humans at Midvale were the ones paid to keep the monsters in check.

Midvale was a vampire facility.

Seemed there were limits to the rights vamps had earned so many years ago when they came out of the coffin. Criminals and crazies, as far as Lucas could tell, didn't have any more rights than cockroaches.

It was shit like this—*this place*—that had forced him to walk away from his job as a detective with the VCU. There was no *real* justice for any paranormal beings, only what the humans wanted them to *think* they had.

No wonder shapeshifters like him remained firmly in the shadows, refusing to let humans know they even existed.

Lucas turned his gaze back to the prisoner. She sat on the concrete floor next to the bolted-down bed, her ankle shackled to the steel frame with a heavy gauge chain strong enough to keep an ox immobile. The weighty links looked ridiculous encircling her slender ankle. Like a Chihuahua wearing a Rottweiler's collar.

From the bed linens to the tank top and loose draw-string pants she wore, everything in the room was gray, faded and cold-looking. The only splotch of color was the girl's hair. The thick, chestnut waves tumbled around her nearly bare shoulders, the ends almost reaching her waist. Her head was tipped down, so that mass of hair obscured her features from his view.

She looked young. Small. Alone.

"Why is she chained to the bed?" Lucas asked. "Seems like overkill in a maximum-security facility."

Vi sighed. "According to Dr. Daniels, she's prone to violent rages. Her behavior is…unpredictable. They keep her under with Thorazine most of the time."

Lucas had seen patients subdued with Thorazine before, but they generally weren't completely catatonic like this one. "They drug her every day? That can't be good for her, right?"

"No, it's not," Violet murmured. She glanced back down at the chart and frowned. "1600 mg a day…that can't be right. I've had two-hundred-pound psychotics that I only gave 800."

Lucas didn't say it, but if she was what they *thought* she was, she was probably three times stronger than the average two-hundred-pound psychotic.

Violet continued skimming the chart, eventually looking like lava might start pouring out of her ears at any moment. "The original dose administered was 200 mg a day, which was a reasonable starting point. Dr. Daniels," she said, spitting out the name with the kind of venom most people reserved for talk of Hitler and flesh-eating bacteria, "increased it by 100 mg a day until she was taking 1,600. No other dose had affected her. Even if she's a *dhampyre*, that much Thorazine could destroy her liver and kidneys. She's lucky to be alive."

Yeah, alive, but gorked out of her mind on Thorazine, chained to a bedframe in the lowest ring of hell. This girl was in *no way* lucky. He ran a hand through his hair in frustration. "Why is she here at all? Humans shouldn't have any idea what she is."

Shit, *he'd* only found out *dhampyres*—genetically engineered half-human, half-vampire hybrids—existed a year ago.

When the woman he loved married one of the fuckers.

"According to Harper's research, she was arrested by the human police for murdering a vamp in Harlem. She, uh…" Vi paused, swallowing hard, "…ripped his head off. Literally. That's when the Harlem Vampire Crimes Unit was called in. Because she's not a vampire, but obviously not human either, they completely avoided the courts and brought her here. All she would tell them when they brought her in was that she worked for Sentry. She didn't even know they'd folded."

The demise of Sentry had been a huge, huge deal in the paranormal community. Sentry had been older than even the most ancient immortals. For centuries, they'd policed paranormal activity, eliminating vampires and shifters and other things that went bump in the night without prejudice. That all changed when vampires came out of the coffin.

Once humans knew about the existence of vampires, all bets were off. Sentry was tried in the court of public opinion and found to be severely lacking. They folded like a cheap card table soon thereafter.

This girl's time with Sentry obviously overlapped with the vamps' big coming out party. She must've been out on assignment when her whole world came crumbling down around her.

And then they locked her up and pumped her full of enough Thorazine to drop an elephant.

And vamps wondered why shifters didn't want humans to know they existed?

"How do we even know this is his sister?" Lucas asked.

Violet adjusted her glasses and smirked up at him. "*He* has a name, you know."

Lucas was well aware that *he* had a name. But speaking the name of the fucker who'd married the woman he loved felt like gargling broken glass, so it was just easier to think of *him* as *douchebag*, or *asshole*.

The luckiest douchebag asshole on the planet. Not that he was bitter or anything. Nope, not at all.

But Violet just continued to throw her all-knowing smirk at him—the kind of smirk that only really smart people could pull off effectively—and waited for him to answer, so he sighed and finally said, "How do we even know this is *Riddick's* long-lost sister?"

Her answering smile was a little annoying. It almost looked like she was proud of him for saying the asshole's name. Well, fuck that noise. He growled at her and she rolled her eyes.

"Geez, chill out," she said, tucking a wayward strand of icy-blond hair back into her complicated-looking up-do. "We don't exactly know this is Grace. Harper's research *suggests* this is her. She wanted to be sure before we told Riddick. Didn't want to get his hopes up."

That sounded like Harper Hall, all right. She'd want to shield her husband from the pain of seeing his sister in a place like this if at all possible. She was always thinking of others first. It was one of the things he loved most about her.

Lucas gave himself a sharp mental slap across the face. *Don't go there, dumbass.*

He cleared his throat. "Fine. What's the plan?"

"I'll talk to her. See if I can get my hands on her complete records, not just the garbage in this file," she said, pinching the file between two fingers and holding it away from her as if it were a bag of steaming dog crap. "Her doctor is a quack. There's more to her hospitalization than meets the eye and I intend to find out what they're hiding. Harper suggested I bring you because she was hoping you'd be able to pick up any scent that might link her to Riddick, you know, genetically."

And he believed that was true. If she was related to Riddick, even a few times removed, he should be able to smell it. Werewolves were talented like that. What he didn't believe was that Harper's motives for sending Violet on this little mission with him were purely practical.

If he knew Harper—and he did—she was trying to be a matchmaker on this one.

People in love always wanted everyone around them to be in love, too. It was a fucking obsession for them. Well, it wasn't happening. Not this time. Not with Violet.

Been there, tried that.

Violet, despite her propensity to blurt out inappropriate comments when she was nervous, was ridiculously adorable, pretty, and charming. And as one of the only shrinks in the state of New York who specialized in treating the paranormal community on an outpatient basis, she was also in a unique position to understand the…complications of his life.

So, in a fit of desperation to move on with his life after Harper gave birth to Riddick's baby—a baby that could've been, *should've* been *his*, damn it—he'd gone out with her on a few dates.

It didn't take long for Lucas and Vi to realize they made better friends than lovers. Besides, Vi was too damn smart and intuitive for her own good. She knew where his head—and heart—were right away and she'd wisely ended things before either of them could get in too deep.

"Fair enough," Lucas said. "Are we doing this here?"

Vi motioned for the guard at the end of the hall. "No. Let's move her to an interrogation room. It's been several hours since she's had any drugs. She should come out of her Thorazine coma soon, I'd think."

In a whisper, she added, "And remember that you're supposed to be a doctor. I don't want anyone to know you have ties to the VCU. It makes people in places like this jumpy."

Well, that shouldn't be a problem. Especially since he *didn't* have ties to the VCU anymore.

The guard fumbled with a ring of keys on his belt as another guard approached with a wheelchair.

One guard waited with Vi in the hall while Lucas pushed the wheelchair to where the girl was sitting. The other guard unlocked the chain on her ankle, then leapt back as if a girl on enough Thorazine to take down a charging rhino could jump up and snap his neck. The other guard looked jumpy as well. All because of a girl who couldn't be more than five-foot-five, or weigh more than one-twenty soaking wet. What a bunch of pussies.

Lucas stared down at the top of her dark head for a moment, not knowing exactly where to grab her in order to get her in the wheelchair. Finally, he slid his hands under her arms and lifted, probably too roughly because she was even lighter than he'd anticipated.

When he tried to ease her into the wheelchair, she surprised him by gripping the lapels of his stolen lab coat in two white-knuckled fists. She lifted her head slowly, her eyes pausing on his chest first, then moving to his throat and chin, and finally, latching onto his.

His breath lodged in his throat. Jesus. She was beautiful. Delicate, knife-edged cheekbones, full pink lips, dark-winged brows, and eyes bluer than any he'd ever seen.

And those eyes were full of pain. If he had to guess by looking into them, he'd say her age could be measured in centuries, even though he knew she was only in her early thirties.

Lucas was accustomed to people needing him. He'd been a cop, for God's sake. People had relied on him for years. But this woman needed him in a different way than anyone else ever had. He could read it clearly in those blue, pleading eyes of hers. This was a matter of life and death. Hers. The protective instincts he'd tried so hard to bury leapt to life in response to her unspoken plea.

He knew some kind of reassuring words were probably in order, but he certainly couldn't find them. At a complete loss for the first time in his life, all Lucas could do was stare down into her eyes, hoping to convey that he would help her any way he could.

Suddenly, her head fell against his chest and she went limp in his grip. He slid one arm around her waist, the other behind her knees, and lifted her as gently as possible. He glanced at the wheelchair, then started for the door without looking back at it again. For some reason, he couldn't make himself put her down just yet.

The guards and Vi parted, letting him pass.

"Um…the wheelchair…"

Vi let her sentence drift off when Lucas shot her a sharp look.

She cleared her throat. “He’s got her,” Vi assured the guards as she hurried after Lucas.

CHAPTER TWO

It took an hour for her to shake off the effects of the Thorazine and look at them with anything resembling comprehension. And as she glanced between Vi, Lucas, and the two armed guards outside the prison interrogation room, she seemed to understand that she'd simply gone from being chained to a bed to being handcuffed at a table.

Not exactly an improvement in circumstances. And she clearly wasn't too happy about it.

Her eyes landed and stuck on what was probably a nice, darkening bruise under Lucas's right eye. He smiled ruefully at her and touched a finger to the place she'd nailed with a flying elbow when he'd finally managed to pull her off the guard she'd been wailing on. "Yeah, you did that," he said, no trace of judgement in his voice.

Hell, he would've done the same if he'd been in her position. Even though he'd most likely have a dandy black eye the next day, he was oddly proud of her for putting up such a valiant fight while still trying to overcome the effects of the drugs pumping through her system.

Beside him, Violet cleared her throat. "It's a common occurrence, I'm afraid. Some patients react…badly when they're coming off certain drugs."

Lucas snorted. Badly? Best he could tell, she'd broken one guard's arm and another's clavicle, in addition to dotting his eye.

She'd reacted like a fucking world-class MMA fighter. It'd been magnificent.

Vi leaned forward. "I'm Dr. Violet Marchand," she said, her voice calm and smooth. It was her I'm-talking-to-a-demented-psychopath voice. Lucas knew it well. She'd used the same tone when she'd dumped him.

The girl jerked her chin in Lucas's direction. "What's *your* name?"

A chill—not a bad one—skated down his spine. Jesus, that was some voice she had. It was the direct opposite of Vi's carefully modulated tones—low, raspy, sexy as all hell.

Vi elbowed him in the gut, snapping him out of his stupor. "Lucas. Lucas Cooper," he answered.

She didn't reply, just continued to shift her gaze between them slowly, methodically, unblinking. He'd seen that kind of careful assessment of a room and a situation before.

Lucas drew a deep breath in through his nose, catching her scent. Hospital-grade soap and laundry detergent. Warm female skin. And beneath all that…

Yep. If her ever-watchful gaze didn't give her away, her scent always would.

He was sitting in front of Noah Riddick's little sister.

When she remained silent, Vi prompted, "Can you tell us your name?"

"Don't have one."

Vi's gaze shifted to Lucas, and he could tell she was thinking the same thing he was. Was the girl weird, crazy, or just being purposefully evasive?

"You don't have one?" Vi asked gently. "What do people call you when they want to get your attention?"

Completely devoid of emotion, she said, "My designation is 754821."

Lucas swallowed a growl. She'd been a prisoner her whole life. Abandoned as a baby by a father who couldn't care less about her, raised and trained by Sentry to do their bidding, then left to rot in this hell hole when Sentry folded. She'd never had a life. Probably didn't even know what a normal life entailed.

Suddenly he wanted to track down every last member of Sentry upper management and beat the ever-loving shit out of them.

When Vi's pointy little elbow jabbed him in the ribs again, he realized he must've growled inadvertently. Shit, if he didn't get hold of himself, he'd wolf-out in front of them and risk ending up in a padded cell of his own.

He gave Vi a nod to let her know he was fine (at least, he *would* be fine) and she turned back to the girl.

"Well," Vi began, her voice shifting to warm and friendly, "754821 doesn't have a very nice ring to it. How about we just call you Seven for now?"

Lucas shot Vi a curious look. Her sharp return look let him know she didn't want to hit the poor girl with the news that she was

Grace Riddick at this point. Whatever. He imagined psychology was a tricky thing, especially in this case.

Seven shrugged. "Fine."

Taking that as a positive, Vi continued, "Why are you here, Seven?"

Seven's gaze moved back to the guards outside the door, then up to the camera above them, before landing on Vi once more. "I killed someone."

Well, at least she was honest, Lucas thought. Most prisoners proclaimed their innocence until the bitter end.

Vi nodded and glanced back down at Seven's file. "Walter Finnley. Can you tell me why you killed Mr. Finnley?"

"It was my job."

"When you worked for Sentry?" Vi pressed.

Seven gave a short nod.

"Do you know why Sentry wanted you to kill him?"

Seven shook her head, but Lucas knew why Walter Finnley was on Sentry's hit list. The fucker had been an ancient vampire with a penchant for draining children. Seven had done the world a favor by offing the bastard. Which brought up another interesting point.

"How'd you manage to kill a centuries-old vampire all by yourself?" he asked.

Those amazing blue eyes narrowed ever so slightly on him. "I was very good at my job. Very good," she said flatly.

He grinned at her. He couldn't help it. Having seen her fight while still under the effects of Thorazine, he'd bet that she'd been a hell of a lot better than just *very good* at her job.

Vi elbowed him again and he turned in his seat to glare at her. "Damn it, woman, that hurts!" he grumbled. "Stop it!"

"We're here to do a job," she hissed back, "not find you a pretty girl to flirt with!"

"I've already done my part of the job," he retorted. "She's exactly who we thought she was. Now we're only waiting on you to finish your job. It's not my fault you're slow as Christmas."

She stuck her tongue out at him, which he thought was pretty damned immature for an Ivy-League-educated shrink, before turning her gaze back to Seven. "So, Seven, you were a slayer for Sentry?"

Seven met Vi's gaze steadily. "No."

Vi glanced at Lucas, her brow knit in confusion. Most humans didn't know much about how Sentry had been organized. Everyone knew they'd used seers (like Harper) to track supernatural threats, and slayers (like Riddick) to eliminate them. But Sentry employed more than just seers and slayers. Empaths were used as interrogators and human lie detectors, and watchers (certified geniuses with a gift for strategy and logistics) helped guide seers and slayers to their supernatural targets.

So, if Seven wasn't a seer, slayer, watcher, or empath, and had been on an assignment to eliminate an ancient vampire when Sentry dissolved, that would mean she'd been a…

Holy shit.

"You were a cleaner," he murmured.

Those blue, blue eyes locked on his. Her expression gave away nothing, but a sudden, slight tension around her mouth and a subtle stiffening of her shoulders gave him his answer.

Vi glanced at him. "What's a cleaner?"

He gave her a very subtle shake of his head. Vi didn't need to know that kind of shit. Hell, he wished *he* didn't know that kind of shit.

Harper's mother, Tina Petrocelli, had been one of Sentry's best and brightest empaths. She'd once told him all about cleaners. Wraiths, she'd called them.

No one ever saw them. They were only called in when everything went bad. When there was a threat no one else could eliminate. A situation no one else had the stomach to deal with. But we all lived in fear of them. If you botched up a job so bad a cleaner needed to be called in, all you could do was take a few deep breaths, pray, and kiss your ass goodbye.

If slayers merely *killed* supernatural threats to humanity, cleaners nuked every trace of their *existence* off the face of the earth, including any unfortunate humans who might have seen too much or knew too much.

Tina was one of the toughest women Lucas had ever known. He had ten inches in height and about a hundred pounds on her, but even he wouldn't want to cross her in a dark alley. And when Tina had told him about cleaners? There'd been fear in her eyes. Genuine, gripping fear.

Anything—or anyone—who scared Tina was not to be taken lightly.

Vi cleared her throat. "And you're aware that Sentry is no longer operational?"

"Yes."

"Who told you?"

"Dr. Daniels."

Lucas frowned at her. Was it his imagination, or did her jaw tighten and her voice get harder at the mention of her doctor?

Vi looked similarly concerned, but let it go to ask, "Did Sentry tell you what you were supposed to do if they were ever shut down?"

Seven's gaze shifted to Lucas. "We were all supposed to die."

Vi and Lucas blinked at her in stereo.

Well. That was a bit of a conversation-stopper, wasn't it?

CHAPTER THREE

Several very pointed questions later (it seemed Seven was no more likely to inadvertently divulge information than her brother—the monosyllabic douchebag), Lucas and Vi learned that in case Sentry was ever exposed to the public, the cleaners were supposed to eliminate each other, one by one. When only one was left, that lucky SOB was supposed to off himself/herself.

A couple of things occurred to Lucas at that point in their conversation. The first was that Seven probably had no idea she was a *dhampyre*, and most likely, neither had Sentry upper management or the other cleaners, seeing as she was *alive* and all. And second…it was entirely possible that Seven's incarceration had saved her life. While the other cleaners were out offing each other *Highlander*-style, Seven was safely locked away in her own private hell.

Maybe she was lucky, after all.

"Do you know anything about your history?" Vi asked Seven. "Your family?"

"My father put me in foster care. I was adopted, then I was sold to Sentry."

Sold. Like farmers sold cattle at market.

Jesus.

But Seven was either a master at masking her emotions or…she just didn't have any. Lucas certainly hoped it was the former. He wasn't willing to leave Seven here, but neither was he willing to drop a sociopath off in the middle of Harper's life, especially with a brand-new baby in the picture. Riddick's sister or not, he couldn't risk little Haven's safety.

Vi opened her mouth to ask another question but was interrupted when a man thrust the interrogation room door open with enough force to rattle the walls.

The guy was around six feet tall, weighed probably two-forty. He had the kind of beefy arms and saggy-around-the-middle appearance that told Lucas he'd been an athlete in his youth. But now, at fifty or so, what had once been muscle had long since degenerated into flab. Intelligence flashed in his cool, gray eyes, though. As did cruelty, Lucas immediately noticed. This was a guy who enjoyed the power he wielded. The illustrious Dr. Daniels, Lucas presumed.

He crossed his arms over his chest and stared down his hawkish nose at Vi. "So, little girl," he began, his gravelly voice adding extra menace to his tone, "you think you can waltz in here and talk to my patient without my permission? The Council will hear about this."

Seven's eyes narrowed on him and she hissed under her breath. Lucas blinked at her, nonplussed. She'd shown absolutely no signs of aggression throughout their entire interview. Until now.

Vi straightened to her full height—which still made her look fun-sized when standing next to a burly guy like Daniels—and shoved her glasses up with her middle finger. Somehow Lucas doubted that particular finger choice had been unintentional.

Anyone who didn't know Violet Marchand might have feared for her safety in a situation like this. But Lucas knew her well. He settled back in his chair and crossed his legs at the ankles. Vi was going to hand this guy his ass in a minute, and Lucas planned to enjoy every minute of it. Too bad he didn't have any popcorn.

"Oh, I don't just *think* it. I *know* I can walk in here and talk to your patient without your permission, Dr. Daniels," she said in her icy-smooth voice, putting just enough derision on his title to let him know she thought it—he—was a joke. "And the Council *already* knows about this. No one told you we were coming because we didn't want to give you a chance to clean everything up and make yourself look respectable. What we've learned—what the *Council* will learn—is that you've been keeping this woman in what amounts to a drug-induced coma for years on a dose of medication that could've killed her."

Shock lit the guy's expression for a split second before his ego took over once again. "*You're* acting on behalf of the Council?"

Lucas winced. The condescension in his tone wasn't going to sit well with Vi. He almost felt sorry for the loser. Almost.

Vi offered Daniels a smile that could cut glass. "The head of the Council? Hunter? I was in his wedding party last month. His wife? Mischa? One of my dearest friends."

The funniest part of that? Other than the shocked-shitless look on Daniels's face? It was an absolutely true statement.

Hunter, a vampire so old he'd had a front-row seat when Christopher Columbus first set foot on American soil, had taken over the Council about two months ago. His wife, Mischa Bartone, was a good friend of Vi's and Harper's, and she also held a power position on the Council.

So, pretty much all Vi had to do was tell her friends she didn't like Daniels, and the dude would be lucky to ever work in his field again. Or, really, in this country. Mischa was a brutal little thing. Lucas could see her banishing Daniels to Siberia for daring to *look* at her friend the wrong way.

But Daniels was either too arrogant or too stupid to realize the precarious ground he was standing on, because he sneered down at Vi and said, "This is *my* hospital. I don't give a shit who you're blowing on the Council. If I tell you to leave my patients alone, you'll damn well do it."

Vi's expression gave nothing away, but Lucas knew her well enough to realize she was moments away from violence, and that wouldn't really do anyone any favors at this point. Even if what he really wanted to do was hold this punk-ass bastard down and let Vi wail on him a little.

Lucas stood up and raised his hands in a placating manner. "Let's just all calm down for a minute." He turned to Daniels and offered his hand. "I'm Lucas Cooper."

He left his arms crossed, eyeing Lucas's hand as if it was covered in dog shit. Then he shifted his gaze, visibly taking Lucas's measure.

Lucas took a moment's pleasure in realizing he was at least two inches taller than this douchebag, and while he didn't outweigh him, he'd be willing to bet he had a good deal more muscle mass. He wouldn't even need to shift to knock this asshole into the dirt. Making a power hungry jerk like this feel small, even in the most literal sense, was truly a gift.

"This is *my* ward," Daniels eventually said, enunciating as if speaking to a foreigner. "And I own everyone in it."

Point taken, Lucas thought wryly. *You're the big, scruffy, insecure dog peeing all over the porch to show the other dogs in the neighborhood who owns the place.*

He let his hand fall to his side. "Let's just dispense with the pissing match, shall we? We've been sent by the Council to assess this patient and determine if her rights have been violated. If everything was as it should've been, we would've left and you never would've known we were here. But now? She'll be leaving with us. Do whatever paperwork you need to do to transfer her care over to Dr. Marchand."

Lucas glanced down at Seven out of the corner of his eye. She hadn't moved or spoken or made a sound, but her eyes tracked Daniels's every move. And in her expression, he recognized an actual emotion for the first time since he'd met her.

Murderous rage.

He had no doubt that if he gave her the room for five minutes, she'd rip him to shreds.

Daniels's lip turned up as he sneered at Lucas. "You vampire rights do-gooders are all the same. Always trying to protect the supernatural freaks. Worried about *humane* treatment for them." He snorted. "What you don't seem to understand is these freaks *aren't human*. They'd rip your throat open and drink you dry if given half a chance."

The hitch in his voice told Lucas that Daniels had personal experience with supernaturals that was anything but pleasant. If he had to guess, he'd say Daniels had lost loved ones to a vampire attack. If he was really the doctor he was pretending to be, he might offer to talk to the man about his issues. But he wasn't a doctor, or even a nice guy, for that matter, so Lucas didn't give a shit about this guy's issues. He was here for Seven.

And besides, Daniels seemed like a complete tool.

Lucas glanced between Seven and Daniels. "I have no doubt she would love to rip *your* throat open. But frankly, she showed no aggression until you came into the room. I think it would be best if you left."

A vein popped out in Daniels's forehead and his complexion took on a tomato-esque hue. He stepped forward until he was toe-to-toe with Lucas. "Maybe you didn't understand me, boy, when I said this is *my* ward. So, I'm not going *anywhere*. Unless," he added, "you think you can force me out."

Lucas smiled. He had no doubt he could force Daniels out of the room. Lucas would love nothing more than to grab him by the graying hair, drive his knee into his nose, and drop him to the ground like the sack of wet shit he was. He cracked his knuckles. "With pleasure."

"Stop!"

Everyone froze and looked back at Seven.

Her eyes remained locked on Daniels. "I have something important to tell you, doctor," she said calmly.

Lucas frowned at the tone of her voice. It was…off somehow. What the hell was she up to?

Daniels straightened his shoulders. "Yeah? What's that?"

"Come closer."

He placed his palms flat on the table in front of her. "Tell me."

She leaned forward until their noses almost touched. "You should have your guards empty the pockets of any guests before you let them in to see prisoners," she whispered.

Lucas's mind reeled and he immediately patted the front pocket of his stolen lab coat. There'd been a pen, a prescription pad, and a paperclip in there. And now, it held…only the prescription pad.

Oh, shit.

But before he could call out a warning, Seven's suddenly uncuffed hands whipped in front of her with inhuman speed, ramming the pen through Daniels's hand, lodging it deep in the table beneath.

As Daniels wailed and tried to pull his hand free, a guard burst into the room, fumbling with his gun, but Seven was faster. She shot over the table and yanked the Glock from his grip, then lashed it across his jaw. He went down hard, cracking his head on the table.

Before he could react, Seven leaped onto Lucas's back like a spider monkey, wrapping one arm around his throat and pressing the barrel of the Glock to his temple. "Move to the door. Now," she hissed in his ear.

"You bitch," Daniels cried, still attempting to yank his hand away from the table. "I'll kill you."

Lucas could almost feel her sneer. "You'll have to catch me first, you son of a bitch."

CHAPTER FOUR

Lucas had never been a hostage before. It was a little disconcerting.

Probably no more disconcerting than it was for Seven to be so much shorter than her hostage that it was necessary to ride him like a palomino out the door. But she probably realized bending him in half to get him down to her level would've slowed her escape. Smart girl.

"Go," Vi said. "I'll take care of this."

He hoped she was referring to getting Daniels to make the guards stand down, rather than taking care of the fucker's hand. But there wasn't really time to discuss much of anything, so he eased the door of the interrogation room open. Shouts and the clang of the ancient alarm system rang out in the hall. Seven's forearm tightened reflexively around Lucas's throat.

"Easy," he muttered. "If I pass out from lack of oxygen, they'll shoot you."

"I'd think that would make you happy," she said, easing her grip enough to keep him upright, but not enough to let the barrel of the Glock slip from his temple.

"I'd rather not see anyone die today. Least of all me."

Three guards suddenly filled the hallway in front of them, weapons drawn. Lucas didn't know their names, but he immediately decided to internally refer to them as Lazy (seriously, the dude had a crazy-looking lazy eye that seemed to be looking straight at his own nose), Hairy (in honor of the dude's visible nose hair, which looked long enough to French braid), and Paunchy (low-hanging fruit, Lucas thought, since the guy looked to be about ten months pregnant).

"Drop your weapons, or I'll blow his head off," Seven yelled.

Lucas sighed. She was either a really good actress, or she was actually willing to kill him. That was disappointing. Why were the pretty ones always crazy? Or in love with someone else?

"Not gonna happen," Paunchy said through clenched teeth. "You might as well let him go."

With her arm still firmly around Lucas's neck, Seven pulled on the Glock's slide and released it. "Do it! Now!"

"Better do as she says," Lucas said. "I do believe she's serious."

The guards eyed each other, then Seven. Finally they laid their weapons on the ground and raised their hands.

"Kick them away," Seven said.

They looked like it was killing them to do so, but they complied. *A good start*, Lucas thought, *but the battle isn't over yet.*

"You," she said jerking her chin toward Lazy. "Call the tower and tell the snipers to stand down. Then call the gate. I want it wide open."

Lucas couldn't help but add, "And for the love of all that's holy, will someone kill that fucking alarm? It's giving me a headache."

Lazy's arm trembled noticeably, but he did as she asked, conveying her demands using the radio clipped to his belt.

The alarm cut off abruptly and the ensuing silence allowed Lucas to hear the rapid thundering of the guards' hearts, and the steady, slow heartbeat of his kidnapper. Interesting.

She jarred him out of his musings by nudging him toward the door. To the guards, she said, "Face down on the floor. Hands behind your heads."

"You'll pay for this, bitch," Hairy jeered as he got down on the floor.

She didn't answer, but Lucas felt her entire body tense as they made their way through another set of double doors and into yet another long corridor. He wrapped his hands around her forearm, partly because he hoped to offer her some measure of comfort, and partly because she was really strong and every time she tensed up, he lost a little more oxygen to his brain.

"You know," he began casually, "we weren't leaving without you. No matter what Daniels said, you were coming with us. Kidnapping me wasn't really necessary."

"I couldn't take that chance."

"I get that."

Her forearm tightened again. "No, you don't," she hissed through obviously clenched teeth. "You have no idea what goes on here. The experiments."

His stomach turned at the thought of what an unscrupulous doctor with a ward full of supernatural mental patients could do when no one was watching. When no one cared. "I won't let anyone hurt you again," he promised. "Neither will Vi."

"Why would you care?"

"Your family sent Vi and me to get you. They want you back."

She snorted. "I don't have any family. And if I did, I doubt they'd want me back. Not now. Not after…"

Not after everything I've done.

Seven hadn't finished her sentence, but Lucas had heard her answer just the same. During his time with the force, he'd interviewed bad people who'd done bad things, and good people who'd done bad things. The bad ones had no remorse, and sometimes no reason for doing what they'd done. The good ones…well, guilt and remorse had been carved into the good ones. It showed in their eyes. Aged them.

Seven had old eyes. The oldest he'd ever seen.

"You're wrong," he whispered. "You do have family. A brother, a sister-in-law, and a niece. They'll love you, no questions asked. They're that kind of people. The best I've ever known."

Her gun hand wavered, then lowered. She slid soundlessly to her feet behind him. He turned around to face her as slowly as possible, not wanting to spook her.

Her brow was knit in confusion as she glanced up at him. "A…brother? *My* brother?"

He nodded. "He's been looking for you. He didn't know you existed until last year, but he's been looking ever since he found out."

She raised a hand and rubbed her temple. "You're not lying," she murmured. "Your heartrate and breathing…they're steady."

"I'm not lying," he confirmed, while thinking, *shit, you can hear that?* He knew *dhampyre* senses were enhanced, but that was ridiculous.

"If I went with you…"

He did a mental fist pump.

"…what would I do? What would my job be? My purpose?"

Great. Now he felt bad for the mental fist pump. The concept of anyone wanting her around just for *her* was completely foreign to her. Her whole life, everyone had wanted something from her.

"Well," he began, "your sister-in-law, Harper, runs a paranormal PI firm. They also do some skip-tracing. I'm sure you could help with that."

That's when he saw another emotion light her eyes. Hope. And damned if it wasn't one of the most beautiful things he'd ever seen.

They stared each other down for another minute. She must've found what she was looking for in his gaze because she handed him the gun, which he quickly pocketed. No need to test their uneasy truce by leaving her armed, he thought.

But their little moment was pretty much decimated as the sound of combat boots pounding across industrial-grade tile heralded the arrival of another guard at the end of the corridor. The guard—a kid who couldn't be more than nineteen—yelled at them to stop and aimed a Glock at them with hands that looked none too steady.

Lucas twisted slightly at the hip so that his body better shielded Seven. "Calm down, kid," he said. "Just turn and go back the way you came and we won't hurt you."

He continued white-knuckling the Glock, his eyes going wide. "I'm not going anywhere and neither are you."

Behind him, Seven sighed and said, "I don't like guns being pointed at me."

Before he could stop her, she reached inside Lucas's jacket, yanked the hunting knife from his belt loop, (*fuck him*, how had she even known that was there?) stepped out from behind him, and flung the blade overhand at the guard's head.

The knife handle—thank God she hadn't tried to kill the hapless little fuck—struck the guard precisely in the center of the forehead. He blinked twice, his eyes crossed, then he passed out cold, falling flat on his back, arms and legs spread comically wide.

But unfortunately, when he fell, he tossed the gun. And because the dumbass hadn't had the safety on, the impact squeezed off a round, which ricocheted off the wall.

Before he could even think about hitting the ground to avoid the ricochet, Seven's hand shot out and fisted an inch in front of his face. Her eyes held his as she opened her palm and let a bullet drop to the floor.

Well…shit. That was unexpected.

Dhampyres couldn't catch bullets with their bare hands.

Lucas grabbed her hand and turned it palm-up, expecting to see raw, ravaged flesh. Her skin was smooth, unmarked, and flawless. He could feel her eyes on him as he traced a line down the center of her palm—where there should be a bloody, gaping hole, damn it—with his index finger.

After a moment of loaded silence, he raised his gaze to hers. "Who the hell are you?" he whispered. But more importantly, he thought, *what* the hell are you?

She blinked at him and pulled her hand out of his, rubbing her thumb into her palm as if she could scrub away all traces of his touch. "I'm Seven."

He nodded, completely nonplussed. "Sure. Okay."

He supposed that was as good an answer as any.

CHAPTER FIVE

Seven took careful stock of her situation, just as Sentry had trained her to do all those years ago.

She refused to let her guard down, but even she had to admit her circumstances had just drastically improved.

Thanks to Dr. Marchand—or, Violet, as she wanted to be called—Seven was officially free of Midvale and wouldn't face any repercussions for hurting Dr. Daniels or any of the guards.

Violet had caught up with them just as they were ready to pull out of the prison's front gate, and from what she'd told Lucas, Seven assumed she'd blackmailed Daniels into letting her go by threatening to expose his illegal and unethical practices to not only the Council, but also the press. Daniels would lose his medical license and face prison time if Violet reported him.

He'd face way worse than that when Seven got ahold of him. And she would. One day, she would. He deserved nothing short of a slow, painful death for everything he'd done to her and so many others behind the rotting walls of that damned prison. And Seven intended to give him *everything* he had coming.

But not today. Today she was going to meet her family.

Family. The whole concept seemed so…surreal to her. She'd always been on her own. Cleaners didn't work with anyone. Didn't form attachments. It was easier that way. Attachments impaired judgement. Created questions that didn't have answers. Questions like *is what I'm doing right or wrong?*

Am I good or evil?

Right and wrong, good and evil…these were things that didn't matter to a cleaner. Watchers could sort out that mess. Cleaners just followed orders. Orders kept everything neat. Uncomplicated.

Most of the time, at least.

But Sentry was gone. She might even be the last living cleaner. She'd have to adapt if she wanted to survive in this new world. Fitting into a family would be a good start.

And if the whole concept of family was strange to her, the idea of her actually *fitting into* a family was damn near unfathomable. Why would a nice, normal family want anything to do with a trained assassin who'd been locked up in a prison's mental ward?

Well, she thought resolutely, she'd just have to treat fitting into her family as an assignment. A mission. She was a good operative. The best Sentry had ever had, by all accounts. She'd just do what she did best. She'd survey the targets. Find out what motivated them and how they operated, learn their schedules, quirks, strengths, and weaknesses. Look for ways to insinuate herself into their lives. Become invaluable. Maybe then they'd accept her. Forgive her for everything she'd done.

Forget what she *was.*

And as it turned out, if Violet was correct, in addition to being a supernatural assassin, Seven was also a *dhampyre*, like her brother. Which explained why she'd been faster and stronger than most of the other cleaners. But according to Lucas, it didn't explain why she could catch bullets with her bare hands.

She glanced up from her seat in the back of the Camry Lucas was driving (she'd bet anything she owned—which was nothing, really—that he would never drive anything as boring as a beige Toyota. The car must belong to Violet.) and looked at him in the rearview mirror.

He was a mystery to her. Violet, she understood. Violet was dedicated to her job and wanted to help as many people as she could. Seven had encountered people like Violet before. They were few and far between these days, but they were out there. Good, decent, nice people. But Lucas? She wasn't so sure he was nice.

He was obviously a shifter. Wolf, if she hadn't missed her guess (and she never, ever missed her guess). The way his eyes flared yellow every now and again when his emotions got the better of him was a dead giveaway. But she didn't sense in him the same general desire to help people she saw in Violet.

So why had he come for her?

Narrowing her eyes, she glanced over to Violet as the two of them made quiet, polite conversation with one another.

The two of them looked good together, she decided. Like they were two halves that would make for an intriguing whole.

Violet was petite and slender with icy blond hair and equally icy pale blue eyes. She was polished, refined, and elegant. But there was also a warmth and compassion in her that naturally put people—even people like Seven—at ease.

Lucas was Violet's antithesis.

His dark blond hair was far removed from his last haircut, and worn in a style that could only be described as disheveled. There was a barely contained, almost feral quality in his eyes that made him look like he was ready for anything. And the way he carried the two hundred or so pounds of lean muscle on his six-foot-two frame let her know he was not only ready for anything, but he could handle himself in any situation. He wouldn't be the type to underestimate an opponent based on size or gender, like so many of the men she'd fought in the past. He wasn't someone she'd want to meet in a dark alley, that was for sure.

And while his eyes were a warm, rich shade of brown that reminded Seven of coffee with just a splash of creamer, they didn't convey Violet's warmth and compassion. In Lucas's eyes Seven saw cynicism. Pain. He'd seen the worst the paranormal community and humanity had to offer and it had shaped him, carved him into a man who was hardened and could be cold. Not unfeeling, but definitely not welcoming. While Violet put her at ease, Lucas made her a little edgy.

But even while he made her a little nervous, Seven couldn't deny he was good-looking. Exceptional-looking, really. She could see why someone like Violet would want him.

Which brought her back to why she imagined Lucas might have helped Violet rescue her from Midvale.

Seven waited for a lull in the conversation before asking, "Are you two having sex?"

Violet had just taken a sip of Diet Coke, and promptly spewed it all over the windshield.

Lucas took one hand off the wheel to brush some of the errant moisture off his shirt sleeve. "Jesus, Vi," he muttered.

"Sorry," Vi sputtered, grabbing a wad of napkins out of the glove box to sop up the mess. "I just wasn't expecting that."

Seven glanced between them, wondering if anyone was going to answer her, or if she'd offended them somehow. She had no idea how to figure out what they were thinking or feeling. Situations like this were exactly why cleaners avoided social contact with normal people.

Lucas caught her gaze in the rearview mirror. "No, we're not," he answered, not sounding at all offended. "Why do you ask?"

Seven tilted her head to one side, studying him. He was telling the truth again. So, he hadn't come after her because Violet asked for his help. "I'm trying to figure out why you're here. Why you'd help me."

"Your brother's wife—your sister-in-law—asked me to find you."

OK, that made sense. And he was telling the truth, but his voice sounded strange when he talked about her sister-in-law. Harper, Violet had said her name was. "Then, are you having sex with Harper?"

Violet barked out a startled laugh and Lucas cursed under his breath.

"No," Lucas said, sounding like he was gritting his teeth. "I'm not."

"Did I ask something I shouldn't have? Is that an…" Seven paused, searching for the right word, "…*awkward* question?"

Lucas opened his mouth to answer, then snapped it shut again. Violet offered her a gentle smile.

"It's a fair question," Vi said. "But you should know that a lot of people do find it awkward to discuss their sex lives. Sometimes to get around that, people might…filter their questions a bit."

Seven leaned forward. Now they were getting somewhere. People had always been uncomfortable around her. Maybe Vi could help with that. "And this *filtering* makes people more comfortable answering my questions?"

Violet nodded. "It can. For example, instead of asking Lucas if he's *having sex* with someone, you could ask him if he's…*seeing* anyone. If he has a girlfriend or wife."

Seemed like *filtering* was very similar to beating around the bush, which she'd never been any good at, either. But, she supposed it was worth a try…

Seven turned back to him, "Lucas, are you—"

"No," he interrupted. "I'm not seeing anyone. No girlfriend, no wife. I came with Violet because Harper asked me to."

Truth.

Then he added, "Harper's a friend. Nothing more."

Seven sat back in her seat and crossed her arms over her chest. Well, that was a first.

He'd just lied to her.

Lots of people had lied to her over the years. People claimed they hadn't seen anything in order to get her to leave them alone. (If she was questioning them, they'd most *definitely* seen something.) People said they weren't scared of her. (They always were.) People told her all the tests and experiments they were running on her wouldn't hurt. (It *always* hurt. Every single time.)

But she quickly found out that having Lucas lie to her felt different than anything she'd ever experienced before.

It made her feel…wait, was this…*sadness*?

No one had ever had enough power over her to make her feel much of anything. She didn't like it. Not one bit.

"Lucas, can I trust you?" she asked quietly, but in a voice sharp enough to separate skin from bone.

He met her gaze steadily in the mirror. "Yes. I'd never hurt you."

Truth.

She nodded slowly. "I guess that's really all I can ask for at this point."

But later? Later was another story.

She'd get the truth out of him eventually. She'd never failed to get a target to talk.

Never.

CHAPTER SIX

Harper Hall Investigations occupied the second floor of a historic brownstone in downtown Whispering Hope. Harper was fortunate enough to own the whole building, and had converted the first floor into a wide, open lobby area. The basement was a full, walk-out apartment unit that Harper rented out.

That basement apartment used to belong to Hunter, but once he took over the Vampire Council with his new wife, they moved into one of the fancy, gated townhouse communities just outside of town where all the homes had windows with special tinted glass, allowing vampires to see and feel the sun without, well, bursting into flames.

After lucking into a parking space right in front of the building, Lucas helped Vi out of the front seat, then opened Seven's door and offered her a hand. She looked at it as if she was expecting an attack.

It'd been a while, but when he was on the force, he'd been known to play a pretty decent "good cop" when interrogating perps. He was out of practice being charming, but he was pretty sure he could still pull it off.

With that in mind, he gave her what he hoped was a reassuring smile. "I'm a Southern boy. Where I come from, gentlemen are raised to open doors for ladies and help them out of cars."

A frown line knit Seven's brow as she took his proffered hand and climbed gracefully—as gracefully as a woman without shoes and blood splatter on her tank top could manage, anyway—out of the car.

"You don't look like a gentleman," she said in the matter-of-fact tone he'd come to appreciate in their short time together.

He couldn't help but bark out a surprised laugh as he took her elbow to lead her into the building. "Don't tell my momma, OK?"

Her frown line deepened. "It's unlikely I'll ever meet your mother. And even if I did, I doubt I'd insult her by saying she'd failed to raise a gentleman."

"Well, that's good, honey. Momma doesn't take kindly to insults. Last time someone tried to mess with me, he ended up in pieces."

Her gaze seemed to stick to his hand at her elbow, as if she wasn't sure why it was there before she lifted her eyes to his. "The shifter genes came from your mother then, I take it?"

"Yes, ma'am."

"Who tried to mess with you?"

Well, shit, he thought. Why was he traveling down this road? It never led anywhere happy. And yet he still heard himself tell her, "My father."

She nodded as if that wasn't shocking at all. He wasn't sure if that was a sad commentary on his life, or on hers.

"Female wolves are very purposeful," she said. "They rarely act violently without clear reason, and usually that reason involves protecting young. I'm sure he deserved it."

Saying a man who'd tried to kill a baby by throwing a sack over his head and tossing him the river—all because he was a shifter and dear old dad was human—*deserved* getting torn limb from limb by a pissed-off momma wolf was probably an understatement.

"Yeah, I guess he did," he said quietly, his voice sounding like he'd gargled with hot coals. Shit, the fact that what that bastard had done so many years ago could still affect him pissed him off to no end.

Seven glanced up at him nervously. "You don't need comfort, do you? I don't have any experience with offering comfort."

He snorted. "No, honey, I don't need comfort. But thanks for asking."

She looked so relieved he almost laughed out loud. He glanced over at Vi, who was biting her lower lip in what he assumed was an attempt to stifle her own laugh.

Lucas gestured toward the overstuffed loveseat in the lobby area. "Why don't you ladies wait here while I have a quick word with Harper?"

Vi nodded her agreement and took a seat, but Seven's eyes narrowed on him. She'd obviously heard something in his words she didn't like. "What's the matter?" he asked her.

She shrugged. "You tell me."

He put his hands on her shoulders and bent his knees a little so he could look her right in the eyes as he said, "It's going to be OK, Seven. I promise you that. Everyone's going to love you."

She returned his gaze with an intensity that almost unnerved him, like she was mentally peeling away the layers of his skin and bone to look directly into his brain. He didn't know what she was looking for, but he assumed she found it because she eventually sat down next to Vi and stopped glaring at him.

He took a deep breath and turned to the elevator before he screwed up with her again.

Seemed like he just couldn't stop himself from fucking everything up with the women in his life.

Lucas's relationship with Harper Hall was complicated on a good day.

And sadly, today wasn't a good day.

Lucas had known Harper for about a year before he ever worked up the nerve to ask her out, and when he finally did, it was already too late. She fell for Noah Riddick almost the moment she set eyes on him. That's just how Harper was. She threw her full heart into everything she did. She knew what she wanted and she went after it. Hard.

It was just his shit luck she hadn't wanted him.

He paused to take a deep breath before letting himself into her office and shutting the door behind him.

Harper's scarred mahogany desk sat in the middle of the room, backlit by the late-afternoon sunlight streaming in through the giant, leaded-glass window that was probably twenty years older than the desk, which was most likely old enough to be considered an antique.

She was standing behind her desk with her back to him, looking out the window. Thank God Riddick wasn't with her. What a relief. Having him here would be the cherry on top of the shit sundae of this situation.

But then she turned around, a smile on her lips, the sunlight playing on her hair, picking out strands of sunny blonde mixed in among brown curls that always looked like they were moving even when they weren't, and he didn't feel relieved anymore.

His gaze fell from her vibrant green eyes to the chubby baby she was cuddling to her chest, and he felt gut-punched by the sight of the two of them together.

So. Fucking. Beautiful.

Harper had the baby sitting upright, facing out, leaning back against her chest. She had one arm wrapped around the baby's chest, and one arm under her butt. The kid's chubby little legs were kicking as if she was on a swing at the park.

Little Haven Hall was only six months old, but she already had an intelligent, mischievous sparkle in her eyes that told Lucas she'd be hard to manage as she got older. Just like her momma.

Haven's eyes were a perfect duplicate of her mother's, but her hair was stick-straight and so black it almost looked blue with the sunlight hitting it. Mom's eyes and dad's hair, he decided. And a little button nose and Cupid's bow mouth that were purely her own. The kid looked like she belonged in a baby food commercial; she was *that* adorable.

Harper jerked her chin toward his face. "What the hell happened to you?"

He touched two fingers to his eye, which was probably swollen from where he'd caught Seven's elbow, and smiled ruefully. "It was…a misunderstanding."

Her nose wrinkled as she took in the rest of his appearance. "You kind of look like Lester right now."

Since Lester was the guy who lived in a refrigerator box behind her building, he didn't take that as a compliment. "Thanks," he said dryly. "You look pretty, too."

She looked way better than pretty, actually.

Motherhood suited her, he decided. She looked…happy. Serene. Settled in a way he was pretty sure he'd never experienced.

And probably never would.

He sat down in one of the chairs in front of her desk and crossed his arms over his chest. "It was her, Harper. She's here."

Harper's eyes widened. "Holy shit! It was really her? Grace? Tell me *everything*."

Lucas gave her a brief rundown of everything that had happened that day, including the altercation with Daniels, and how Violet had suggested calling her Seven, at least for now. When he was done, Harper looked shell-shocked.

"Jesus," she muttered. "How the hell am I going to keep Riddick from storming that place and ripping Daniels's arms off?"

Lucas wasn't sure, since he'd pretty much used every ounce of strength he had not to do the same thing to the guy. And Riddick? Well, self-control wasn't exactly one of his virtues.

"I don't think he'll have to do anything to Daniels," Lucas said. "Violet already called Mischa. The Council is probably at the prison right now, collecting all of Dr. Frankenstein's notes and shutting down his ward. And if I know Mischa, she'll have his medical license pulled, and will most likely press charges against him for his treatment of the patients."

Harper's answering smile was as beautiful as it was terrifying. "Oh, I'm sure she won't stop at just that. Mischa's a pit bull. She won't let go of the bastard's balls until they fall off in her hand." In her best Mr. Burns voice, she added, "Excellent."

Mental note: do not get on Harper and Mischa's bad side.

Lucas shifted uncomfortably in his seat. "Well, as lovely as that mental image is—and thanks *ever* so much for that—I just wanted to prepare you before meeting her. Didn't want you to be too surprised."

Harper frowned. "Why? What's wrong with her?"

"Nothing. She's just…unique." He couldn't help but smile a little at *that* understatement. "And she's not used to being around people. You and your crew should probably dial back your natural...exuberance when you're first meeting her."

Harper cocked her head to one side and gave him a speculative smile that made him no less uncomfortable than her bloodthirsty smile. “You like her,” she said.

This was obviously a trap. If he said no, he was lying and Harper would realize it, then read too much into it. If he said he *did* like Seven, Harper would read too much into it. Talk about a fucking double-edged blade.

“Whatever,” he mumbled. “I just don’t want you freaking her out. She’s been through a lot.”

He was spared whatever smartass comment Harper was sure to make by Riddick, who let himself into the office, and without a word or so much as a glance in Lucas’s direction, stalked up to his wife and planted a kiss on her that visibly weakened her knees.

When he pulled back, he smiled down at her and said, “Missed you today, Sunshine.”

She licked her lips and blinked up at him a few times before saying, “I guess so.”

Haven started making little grunting noises, actively protesting not being the center of her father’s attention. She started waving her little arms at him, making grabby motions with her hands, all while scrunching her face up to clearly convey her annoyance. Lucas couldn’t help but smile. For a little person who hadn’t yet mastered verbal communication, Haven certainly had no trouble expressing herself.

"I know, I know," Riddick said, easing Haven out of her mother's arms and cuddling her against his chest. "I missed you too, pretty girl."

When Riddick kissed her on the top of her head, she laid her cheek on his shoulder, stuck her finger in her mouth, and let out a happy sigh. It was the first time Lucas had ever seen her not fidgeting and squirming and kicking.

Harper shook her head at her husband, hands on her hips in annoyance. "How do you do that? She's never that still for me."

He shrugged and smiled down at her until she smiled back, her annoyance all but forgotten.

Lucas waited for the pain to level him. After all, here he was with a front-row seat to the kind of love and happiness and contentment he'd always wanted, watching the woman he'd thought was *the one* gaze up at a man who wasn't him. A few months ago, the sight would've driven him right into a bottle of Glenlivet to drown his sorrows. He kept waiting for the negativity and bitterness to drag him under. And waiting. And waiting…

But seeing the way they looked at each other at that moment? As if they needed each other more than they needed oxygen? Lucas realized he couldn't hate Riddick anymore for grabbing hold of Harper with both hands and never letting go. Together they were this perfect team, two halves of a whole.

And it wasn't like he'd never had his shot. Shit, he'd known Harper first. He could've asked her out long before Riddick ever showed up on the scene. But something had held him back.

Something had *always* held him back in all of his relationships. Kept him from fully committing.

Vi had asked him something when she dumped him that always stuck with him.

Am I the last person you think about before you go to bed at night, and the first you think of in the morning, Lucas? Do you wonder what I'm doing or thinking when we're not together?

Feeling like the biggest dick in the world, he'd had to tell her no. But in true Vi fashion, she'd simply nodded and admitted she didn't feel that way about him, either. It'd been the most mature breakup of his life. No tears, no muss, no fuss. At the time, he'd assumed he didn't feel that way about Vi because he was in love with Harper. But now he was starting to think…

"Holy shit," he blurted. "I don't love you! I never did."

Harper and Riddick both swiveled in his direction, heads cocked in confusion. Harper eventually said, in a tone dryer than Sahara sand, "Well, that bordered on rude, Lucas. I guess that's payback for saying you looked like Lester?"

Lucas face-palmed when he realized how that must have sounded. "No, that's not what I meant. Of course I love you. I mean, you're *you*," he said, gesturing to, well, all of her. "Everyone loves you. I'm just not *in love* with you." He groaned. "Jesus, now I sound like a teenage girl in one of those fucking *Twilight* movies."

Riddick shifted Haven higher on his shoulder and frowned at Lucas before glancing down at Harper. "I'm not sure how I should be taking this. Logically, I think I should be happy. But for some reason, my gut's telling me I should be beating the shit out of him." He shrugged. "I don't know, babe. Just tell me what you want me to do and I'll do it."

Harper tapped on her lower lip with her index finger like she was thinking about it before saying, "Well, his knowledge of the *Twilight* movies does seem like a beatable offense." Her eyes practically glittered with mischief. "But I think we can leave him un-maimed this time."

Since Riddick still looked like he could go either way on beating the shit out of him, Lucas decided to keep his mouth shut while his brain processed the fact that he'd never actually been *in love* with Harper. He'd been attracted to her, of course, but what he really wanted was what she had with Riddick. That partnership, the closeness. Family.

Goddammit, he'd wasted a lot of time buried in a bottle, feeling sorry for himself for no good reason.

Which for some reason brought his thoughts immediately back to Seven.

"Shit, Riddick, did you come up here from the lobby?"

"No. Fire escape."

Lucas couldn't help but raise a brow at that one. Harper rolled her eyes and said, "Sometimes there're clients in the lobby. Riddick dealt with some clients when I was on bedrest." She gave her husband a stern look. "Let's just say they aren't clients anymore. We've decided it's best for Riddick to avoid direct client contact whenever possible."

"It's not my fault some people don't want to hear the truth," he grumbled.

Harper snorted. "There's a way to tell someone you won't take their surveillance case without calling anyone a—," she paused, making air quotes with her fingers, "'fucking pathetic stalker.'" Her brows flat lined. "Some people find that off-putting."

He kissed Haven's head again, looking completely unrepentant, before turning back to Lucas. "So why do you care if I came up through the lobby?"

Harper looped an arm through Riddick's and smiled up at him. "Because we have a visitor. A very *special* one."

Lucas held back a smirk. They had no fucking idea just how special. But they were about to find out.

CHAPTER SEVEN

The woman called Harper—her sister-in-law, Seven reminded herself—was a hugger. Violet had barely finished an introduction before Harper grabbed Seven and hugged her with a surprising amount of strength for a human woman who was only five-six and couldn't weigh more than a hundred and thirty pounds.

Since she was fairly certain she'd never been hugged in her life, Seven wasn't exactly sure what proper hug etiquette was. Was she supposed to hug Harper back? If so, where did her arms go? Around the neck? Around the waist? There were just too many variables. Ultimately, Seven decided it was safest to just stand there, arms at her sides, and wait for the hug to be over.

The vampire couple, Mischa and Hunter, weren't huggers. But they did shake her hand and were polite enough to pretend to not notice the shiver that ran through her as their power washed over her in waves. If they'd been one of her Sentry assignments, she was pretty sure she wouldn't be able to take one of them out, let alone both.

Hunter smirked at her, letting her know that a) she wasn't wrong, and b) he could read her mind. Good to know. She immediately threw up her mental shields, just as Sentry had taught her so many years ago.

The two of them together was an odd sight. They were polar opposites—he was over six feet tall, she was barely five-two, he was obviously of Native American descent, she appeared to be Italian American—and yet somehow, they looked perfect for each other.

Seven eyed his features critically for a moment to determine which tribe he'd most likely belonged to before saying, "*Háu.*"

He jerked back in surprise. "You speak Lakota?"

She thought that was a strange question. Of course she spoke Lakota. Wasn't that obvious? "*Tóš*," she replied, completely unnecessarily, in her opinion.

Mischa cocked her head to one side. "Do you speak other languages, too?"

"Yes."

Mischa and Harper exchanged an odd glance before Harper asked, "How many?"

"All of them."

That seemed to give everyone pause, so Seven didn't offer any further explanation. She supposed it wasn't relevant that as a cleaner, she'd been required to travel extensively and survive in any culture, anywhere. Her Lakota was rusty and limited, as she'd never had much opportunity to practice using it.

A small wererat/vampire hybrid named Benny lounged against Harper's desk. He was a friend who also did some freelance work for the firm, Harper told her. He made no move to hug her or shake her hand, but his gaze widened when she jerked her chin in his direction to acknowledge his presence.

"Holy shit," Benny said. "You're the hottest woman I ever seen outside of porn movies."

Seven had no idea how to respond to that, so she didn't. Harper, however, had no problem slapping Benny on the back of the head with an open palm. "You really want to sexually harass Riddick's sister? And besides, there are three other women in the room, Benny. It's rude to point out that one is prettier than the others."

Benny shook his head. "Nah, I never said she was prettier. But there are different kinds of hot, you know? See, you're *girl-next-door* hot. *Approachable* hot." He gestured to Mischa. "Hotness over there is *exotic* hot. The good doc over there," he made a sweeping gesture in Violet's direction, "is *icy* hot."

Violet rolled her eyes. "Great," she mumbled. "I'm the over-the-counter ointment of the group."

Benny ignored her, gesturing instead to Seven. "And *she*, is *scary* hot. Like she could hurt me and I wouldn't even care because she's so hot. The only place you usually see scary hot chicks is in porn movies."

"Well then, now that you've explained, it all makes perfect sense," Harper said.

But her tone, Seven noticed, implied the direct opposite. She didn't have much experience with sarcasm, but something told her Harper was a master of it.

Riddick—her brother—came back from putting the baby down for a nap in the nursery, which was really just the office next to Harper's. Harper smiled at him and asked, "Was she tired?"

He nodded. "Out like a light the minute I laid her down."

Seven found it hard to stop looking at Riddick. It was obvious they were related. They had the same complexion and eye color. The same high, sharp cheekbones.

But beyond the physical similarities, they also shared a hardness in the eyes she had to assume came from being a *dhampyre* who'd worked for Sentry. Riddick was a man who'd done his fair share of killing. He probably had regrets, just like she did. She wondered if he had nightmares, too.

Like her—and unlike his wife—Riddick wasn't terribly touchy-feely. But she saw the emotion in his eyes when he looked at her. Lucas had been right. Riddick was glad to have her with him.

As her thoughts drifted to Lucas, so did her eyes. He was standing in the doorway of Harper's office, leaning a shoulder against the doorjamb, arms crossed over his chest. Anyone who didn't know better would assume he was a casual observer, not really invested in what was going on in the room. But Seven knew better.

Every time she felt out of sorts or unsure of how to behave, she'd look to Lucas and find him watching her. He'd give her the barest hint of an encouraging smile and she immediately felt calmer, more like herself.

It was disconcerting that someone—especially someone she'd just met—had that kind of power over her. The only reason she'd managed to stay alive so long was because she'd always been in control of her emotions and actions. She was a cold, calculating, strategic thinker. Until today.

Today she was somebody's sister, aunt, and sister-in-law. Today she was someone who could feel a man's gaze on her from across the room. Someone who could still feel the heat of his skin against hers from when he'd helped her out of the car earlier.

Someone who'd liked that feeling far more than she ever would've expected.

Riddick stopped in front of her and laid a hand lightly on her shoulder. "Are you OK? I'm sure this is all a little overwhelming."

Overwhelming was a good word for it. As if she was drowning in three feet of water in plain sight of the shore. Her eyes drifted back to Lucas before meeting Riddick's. "I'm fine." She searched her brain for a moment, wondering what else she should say. What would normal people say? She finally settled on a simple "Thank you."

His answering smile was sardonic, as if he knew she was full of shit and just telling him what he wanted to hear, but he didn't call her out on it. Instead he brushed the knuckles of one hand whisper-soft over her cheek, the gesture so tender and so completely foreign to Seven that she felt a lump forming in her throat.

"Oh, shit, I can't stand it," Harper blurted before shoving Riddick out of the way and grabbing Seven in another bone-crushing hug. "We're just so happy to have you here!"

Suddenly it all became too much. The lump of emotion in her throat, a tearful Harper in her arms, everyone looking at her, smiling and happy…it was just too much. Her heart rate and breathing kicked up until she felt lightheaded.

Of their own volition, her eyes sought out Lucas, who seemed to understand her unspoken plea. He immediately pushed away from the doorframe and pried her out of Harper's arms. "OK, OK," he murmured. "Give her some air, Harper."

Harper nodded, eyes glistening. "Sorry. I'm just really happy for you both. I'll stop the hugging." She twisted her fingers up into some kind of complicated-looking knot. "Scout's honor."

Benny snorted. "Like you were ever a Scout."

"I was too a Scout," Harper said, indignant.

Mischa rolled her eyes. "You were banned for life after the first cookie sale for giving Amy Sparacino a swirly. I don't think that counts."

Harper flipped her hair and waved a hand dismissively. "Nuance. I was there. I had the uniform and everything. That totally counts."

Seven breathed a huge sigh of relief as Harper, Benny, and Mischa continued to banter back and forth. With the focus off her, she could relax again.

Lucas put his hands on her shoulders and eased her back against his chest. His heat and strength enveloped her, as did the clean, woodsy, masculine scent of his skin. She fought the urge to turn in his arms and bury her nose in the space where his neck met his shoulder. That kind of reaction probably wasn't normal, she decided. He was just trying to offer comfort, after all. Nothing more.

Violet cleared her throat. "Seven, I'm sure that Mischa and Harper keep some clothes here in case you'd like to clean up and change."

Mischa nodded. "In the hall closet behind the reception desk, I keep some sweats and hoodies. You're welcome to whatever you'd like."

Harper added, "I have some stuff in there, too. Shoes, too. We look like we're close to the same size."

Seven glanced down at her institutional-grade tank top and pants. They were still serviceable. "These are fine."

Violet shifted from one foot to the other, looking uncomfortable. "But…aren't you cold?"

She'd been trained to work in any environment. She could run ten miles, uphill, barefoot in the snow if she had to. "No. I'm fine."

As everyone continued to look uncomfortable, another thought occurred to Seven. "Were you just trying to get me to leave so you could talk about me?"

Harper barked out a sharp laugh and Riddick grinned at her.

Violet sighed, looking dismayed. "Was I that obvious?"

Seven shrugged. "Subterfuge isn't for everyone. You shouldn't feel too bad about it."

Harper grinned at her. "You and me? We're gonna get along just fine."

CHAPTER EIGHT

"OK, so why the fuck are we calling her Seven instead of Grace? It's just fucking weird."

Violet pinched the bridge of her nose and sighed, obviously unaccustomed to having her recommendations questioned. "Riddick, I understand this is difficult, but that girl is simply not ready to be *Grace* yet. *Grace* comes with expectations. You expect *Grace* to be part of your family, a long-lost sister, aunt." She paused, shaking her head. "That's a lot to live up to for someone who isn't used to being around people at all. *Seven* can just be *Seven.* No expectations, no preconceived notions. If she decides she wants to be *Grace* one day, that'll be up to her."

"It's still fucking weird," Riddick muttered.

Harper slipped an arm around his waist. "Whatever is best for her is fine with us, right?"

He sighed. "Yeah. Of course."

Benny rubbed the back of his neck. "I hate to be the one to shit in your Cheerios, Riddick, but how do we know she's, uh, not dangerous? I mean, I crossed paths with a cleaner once back in the day, and man, that dude was fucking *nuts.*"

Riddick growled and took a menacing step toward Benny before Harper tugged him back to her side.

Lucas took a few deep breaths to control his own irritation with Benny for asking such a thing before saying, "She's not dangerous. She could've killed me, Vi, Daniels…hell, she could've killed every guard in that place today and she didn't. After what they did to her…" he trailed off, taking a few more deep breaths. "Everyone is fine. She wasn't ever out of control."

Hunter raised a brow at him. "Not ever? Your black eye is telling a different story. I'm sure there's a doctor and at least a few guards at Midvale who'd disagree as well."

Mischa frowned at him. "She was defending herself. If I'd been in her place, I probably would've done the same thing."

Hunter chuckled. "My love, I have no doubt they would have been begging for mercy had you been in Seven's place. But that's not my point. My point is that after what she's been through, I don't think anyone here can evaluate how dangerous she may or may not be. You have to face the possibility that she could be…broken, for lack of a better term."

"Bullshit," Lucas spit out. "She's not *broken.* Talk to her for five minutes and you can see that. She's strong and smart. She's a fighter."

"Strong and smart people can be dangerous, too, man," Benny added nervously.

"She's not dangerous," Lucas said through gritted teeth.

Hunter, still annoyingly calm, asked, "Are you willing to stake your life on that?"

"Yes," he said without hesitation.

"And Haven's life?"

Well, that let the steam out of his argument right quick. Fuck.

Everyone got quiet after Hunter dropped that little bomb on them.

Vi was the first to speak up. "Look, I don't think she's an immediate threat to anyone. She understands the difference between right and wrong. She doesn't want to hurt anyone, except Dr. Daniels, and honestly, I can't fault her for that one. But she *does* seem to struggle with empathy."

"Like sociopaths," Benny mumbled, then swallowed hard when both Riddick and Lucas shot damn-near lethal glares in his direction.

Vi hastened to add, "She understands the *concept* of empathy, which is a good start. In that respect, she's like a child. She'll need to be taught how to understand and react to the emotions of others. I'm recommending she come to therapy with me, twice a week, for the foreseeable future."

"Has anyone thought through the logistics?" Mischa asked. "Where's she going to stay? Does she even have…anything?"

"I'll get her whatever she needs," Riddick said.

Harper bit her lip. "That's fine, but we don't have an extra bedroom. She could sleep on the couch in the living room, but that wouldn't be very comfortable, especially with Haven waking up every 4 or 5 hours to eat."

"I got an extra room," Benny offered. "She can—"

"No," Riddick and Lucas interrupted in unison, then frowned at each other while Harper chuckled at them.

Benny sighed. "It was the porn comment, wasn't it?"

"That, and you live in a crack den," Mischa said with an eye roll. "I wouldn't want her to *visit* your place let alone *live* there. No offense."

Benny matched her eye roll, and added a snort. "Yeah, how could I possibly be offended by that, Hotness?"

"What about you, Misch?" Harper asked. "You guys have an extra room."

Mischa glanced up at Hunter and bit her lip before addressing Harper. "I didn't get a chance to tell you, but the adoption agency approved our application."

Handshakes, back-slapping, and hearty congratulations ensued. Lucas stayed out of it. He knew how the adoption process worked and what Mischa was really trying to say. Anyone living in their house would have to submit to a thorough background check. And Lucas couldn't think of a single agency that would be cool with giving a baby to a vampire couple who lived with an ex-Sentry cleaner who just happened to also be a longtime guest in a prison mental ward.

"What about you, Vi?" he asked when the happy baby chatter died down.

Vi shook her head. "If she's to be my patient, I need to be a neutral party. Someone she can talk to about anything without fear of judgement. If she's living with me, dependent on me for a roof over her head, she won't be able to speak freely with me."

Riddick ran a hand through his hair in frustration. "We'll have to find her an apartment. In the meantime—"

"She'll stay with me."

Lucas blinked. Shit. Had he said that out loud? Judging by the shocked looks on everyone's faces, he guessed he did.

Riddick's eyes narrowed on him. "Why would she stay with *you*?"

The emphasis he put on the word "you" was insulting. Lucas had a nice house—a four-bedroom ranch—in a safe neighborhood. It's not like he had a criminal record or a heroin habit or anything. There were definitely *worse* guys Riddick could entrust his sister to, for fuck's sake.

There were certainly *better* guys, too. But Lucas saw no point in bringing that up.

"Well, the rest of you aren't offering up any solutions, just more problems," Lucas said, jaw clenched. "Besides, she trusts me. In the short term, she'll probably be more comfortable with me than with any of you."

Riddick opened his mouth to protest, but Vi cut him off. "He's probably right," she said. "At the prison, Lucas got her to open up better than I could've. He was the one who got her out of her cell. In her mind, he rescued her. It's not surprising that she's developed a bit of a…bond with him."

Shit, the way she said "bond" sounded really dirty for some reason. He hoped no one else picked up on that.

Lucas clapped his hands together. "Great. It's settled. I'll let her know."

He ignored the murmurs behind him as he made his way to the door, stopping only when Riddick laid a hand on his shoulder.

"Just be sure you don't *bond* too much with my sister," Riddick said in a menacing voice, low enough that only Lucas could hear.

Yep. Riddick had picked up on the unintentional dirty comment as well. He should reassure the guy that he understood how much Seven had been through, and that he had no intention of taking advantage of her when she was so clearly in crisis. That's what a gentleman would do.

Lucas clapped Riddick on the shoulder bro-style. "I haven't really had a quality *bond* in a while, if you get my meaning," he said, conspiratorially. "And she *is* scary hot…" he paused, pretending to think it over. "But for you? After all you've done for me? I'll do my best, man. No promises, though."

And with that parting shot, he left the office to find Seven.

Guess he wasn't much of a gentleman after all.

He did his best not to laugh as Riddick cursed under his breath and muttered something about ripping Lucas's arm off. At least he *thought* Riddick was talking about his arm.

Yeah, being a gentleman was *totally* overrated.

CHAPTER NINE

Seven sensed he was behind her before he even said a word. Even if she was blindfolded, she could pick him out of a crowd based on nothing but the wild, raw energy and heat that rolled off him. She'd certainly never noticed that with any other shifters she'd encountered over the years. Maybe it was just a *Lucas* thing.

Lucas moved in close behind her to look over her shoulder. "What are you doing?"

Seven shushed him. "You'll wake her."

When she left the room so everyone could talk about her, she changed into Harper's spare clothes—Mischa's were way too small for her—then found herself in Haven's nursery.

Haven had been asleep, one arm thrown up over her head, little snuffling snores occasionally escaping her open mouth. In her other fisted hand she clutched a fluffy…*thing* that had a teddy bear head and a small blanket for a body. It looked pretty strange to Seven, but the way Haven held it possessively against her cheek told her this was one of the child's most prized possessions.

At one point, Haven snored loud enough to startle herself awake, and Seven found herself gazing down into the most beautiful green eyes she'd ever seen. A little frown line appeared between Haven's brows and Seven prepared herself for the scream the child was surely going to let loose. After all, there was a total stranger standing over her crib, watching her sleep. Who wouldn't scream under similar circumstances?

But after a moment of intense eye contact, Haven's frown line disappeared, and she offered Seven a wide, drooly, toothless grin. Seven was so stunned she couldn't even bring herself to smile back.

Haven dropped her teddy bear blanket and reached for Seven's hand, which was curled around the edge of the crib. The annoying lump of emotion Seven had been choking down all day reappeared with a vengeance as she moved her hand close enough that Haven was able to latch onto her pinky.

Haven pulled Seven's hand to her cheek and held it there, just as she'd held her precious teddy bear blanket. And with a deep, contented sigh, she fell back to sleep.

It was the most *acceptance* Seven had ever known.

That had been about twenty minutes ago. She'd been standing there ever since, unmoving, watching Haven sleep the kind of deep, peaceful slumber Seven was pretty sure she'd never experienced in her life. The kind of sleep only someone who was loved and wanted and cherished could ever have. It was the sleep of innocence, of purity.

If her mother had lived, would she have dressed baby Seven—or rather, baby *Grace*—in fleece footie sleepers with little cartoon ducks on them and tuck her in for naps with a cuddly teddy bear blanket?

She felt Lucas's breath on the back of her neck as he chuckled, and she shivered.

"She's really got a hold on you, doesn't she?" he said quietly.

If any other man had dared to get this close to her, she would've driven an elbow back into his gut to move him out of her personal space. But with Lucas? His nearness didn't bother her. Quite the opposite, in fact.

She'd only been part of a family for a few hours and she was already losing her edge. Great.

"She woke up a little while ago and smiled at me," she said.

"Maybe she recognizes you're family." His voice took on a teasing note as he added, "Or, maybe she's a sucker for a pretty face, just like her Uncle Lucas."

He thinks I'm pretty.

Seven quickly tamped down the fluttery, girly feeling in her gut his casual statement had unleashed. Being pretty was nothing to be proud of. The arrangement of her features was nothing more than random genetics at work.

Besides, the fact that they found each other attractive didn't mean anything. Men like him surely didn't have relationships with women like her. And even if they did, what the hell did she know about being in a relationship? It was highly unlikely she'd ever find the kind of love Riddick and Harper shared.

"It just as easily could've been gas," she said, ignoring the pain in her chest at the thought of never knowing what it felt like to have someone look at her like Riddick looked at his wife.

Damn it all to hell. She was *definitely* losing her edge.

"See, I never understood why people say that. Why would anyone smile because of gas?"

Seven thought about it for a moment, then frowned. "That logic does seem flawed, doesn't it? Why do people say that?"

"No idea. People are mostly a mystery to me."

Seven gently shifted Haven's grip back to the teddy bear and slid her hand out of the crib. She turned to face Lucas, expecting him to step back. He didn't.

Well, she thought, if he expected her to retreat, he'd be sorely disappointed. She'd never backed down from a challenge in her life. It was one of the few things Sentry had taught her that might actually be useful in this new life of hers.

Standing so close that if she took a deep breath, her breasts would touch his chest, she tipped her head back to meet his gaze. "Am I a mystery to you, too, Lucas?"

His eyes dropped to her mouth, and she felt her heart rate kick up a few notches. "You are most definitely a mystery to me, beautiful."

She let her own gaze drop to his mouth. His lips looked soft. What would they feel like under her own? "Then why are you letting me stay with you?"

He sighed. "Heard all that, did you?"

"I have excellent hearing."

"I'll remember that," he murmured.

"Why did you stand up for me in there?" she pressed. "Why would you let me into your house, into your life? You could've just dropped me off at Riddick's doorstep and walked away. Why didn't you?"

His eyes roamed over her features for a moment before returning to hers. "I…don't know."

His heart rate and breathing were accelerated. "Liar," she hissed.

He grabbed her wrist when she tried to step around him. Without thought, she twisted her hand around and grabbed his wrist. One pull and quick pivot later and he was on one knee at her feet, arm twisted behind his back.

And wasn't *that* just a perfect way to say thank you to someone who had rescued her from hell and agreed to take her into his home?

Way to blend in, Seven, she chastised herself. Way to blend.

"Shit," she muttered, releasing his arm. "I'm sorry. I…wasn't thinking."

He slowly climbed to his feet, rubbing his wrist, which, she was horrified to discover, was a bright, violent red from where she'd twisted it.

"First of all," he said, sounding incredibly calm for someone who'd almost had his wrist broken, "don't *ever* apologize for that. That was fucking *awesome*."

Her eyes shot to his face, and his grin was as beautiful as it was vexing. "How can you say that? I could've hurt you," she said, a hitch in her voice.

"Yep. And you didn't. You showed control and restraint. Hell, if half the women in this city could do what you just did, there'd be a shit-ton fewer instances of domestic violence, I can promise you that. Don't apologize for being a badass."

She certainly didn't feel very *badass* at the moment. She hadn't had much cause to feel embarrassed over the years and she couldn't say she particularly enjoyed the feeling now.

"I'm not used to having people touch me," she whispered. "When Harper hugged me? It just felt all wrong. I didn't even know where to put my hands."

Half expecting him to laugh at her pathetic admission, she avoided eye contact. But after a moment of loaded silence, he surprised her by opening his arms to her.

"I can help with that," he said.

The low, growly tone of his voice sent a shiver down her spine. "You're not afraid of what I might do?"

His smile was warm. The look in his eyes? Infinitely warmer. "No," he said without hesitation.

Truth.

Well, it wasn't like the thought of being in his arms was abhorrent in any way. And if she was to fit into this family, she couldn't very well go around breaking wrists every time someone laid a hand on her. Time to move on from the Sentry way of life.

Drawing in and releasing a deep breath in an effort to stanch her restless energy, she took a step toward him. He just waited patiently, arms open.

One more step had her close enough that she could once again feel his body heat. That, in combination with his scent—

laundry detergent, soap, and warm male skin—was the last bit of reassurance she needed. Leaning forward, she rested her forehead on his chest, but left her arms hanging at her sides.

No need to rush it, right?

She closed her eyes as his hands brushed over her shoulders, then slowly slid down her arms before finally pulling her in closer. When she was pressed tightly against him, his arms banded around her lower back.

Seven breathed deeper and for the first time in, well, maybe *ever*, she felt all the tension drain from her body. With one gesture, Lucas was able to do something none of the people in the other room were able to do, even though they'd obviously tried their best.

He made her feel like she *belonged* somewhere.

Here, in Lucas's arms, she wasn't a mistake, a weapon, a freak. She was just…Seven.

And right now? Being Seven didn't feel like such a terrible thing to be.

Holy hell but she felt good in his arms.

Despite her fragile mental state—shit, despite *his* fragile mental state—and despite all sense of reason, which told him not to get involved with Riddick's sister, Lucas's thoughts wandered to what it would feel like to be in a long-term relationship with someone other than Harper.

He'd never had anything but shit luck with his past relationships. But something about Seven made him willing to try it all again.

You just met her, he reminded himself. *That kind of thinking makes you sound like a fucking stalker. Slow the hell down.*

True. It was all true. But that didn't mean he couldn't appreciate how perfectly her body fit against his. Or how amazing the clean, simple scent of soap smelled on her skin.

He rested his cheek on top of her head, marveling at how soft her hair was. She still hadn't moved a muscle. He knew he should let her go, but he couldn't bring himself to do it just yet.

And that's when she slid her arms through his to wrap around him. Delicate, tentative fingers fisted around his shirt at his back. A shuddering sigh escaped her as she relaxed against him, and that one little gesture of trust from her was almost enough to bring him to his knees.

What the hell was it about this girl that drew him to her in a way no one had in a really long time? Was it empathy for what she'd been through, or was there more to it than that?

"Is a hug supposed to feel this good?" The whispered words, spoken so quietly even his supernatural hearing had trouble hearing them, pulled him from his thoughts.

He pressed a quick kiss to the top of her head. "Only when you're doing it right."

She pulled back and studied him with those old, old eyes. Eyes that had seen way more they should've in such a short life. "Thank you."

Reluctantly, he let her go. "Anytime, beautiful. Hugs and daring rescues," he joked, trying to rein in his emotions. "That's what I'm here for."

She cocked her head to one side, and he knew in an instant that his joking around wasn't fooling her. "Is it?"

"No," he murmured. "That's not really what I'm here for."

"Then why are you really here, Lucas?"

"I'm here for you. Only you."

He blinked, shocked by his own admission. Apparently he'd been hanging out with Vi and the completely filter-less Harper for too long, because he'd blurted that out without even thinking about it. It was a truth he'd been struggling to figure out how to explain to her when she accused him of lying earlier. Seemed he'd been overthinking the whole thing.

"Truth," she whispered.

Then she did something he'd never seen her do before, and the beauty and power of it almost knocked the air right out of his lungs.

She smiled.

Her whole face lit up when she smiled, driving the haunted shadows from her eyes. It was like watching the fucking sun rise over the horizon at dawn. He swallowed hard.

I'm. So. Fucked.

CHAPTER TEN

Lucas lived in the suburbs about ten minutes away from downtown Whispering Hope.

Seven bounced her leg restlessly, gnawing on her thumbnail as she eyed his house through the passenger-side window of his beat-up, late-model F150. (She'd just *known* the beige Camry couldn't have been his!)

It was a ranch-style, brick-and-river-rock house that looked to have been built in the seventies. The oversized windows were trimmed in unpainted cedar, and fat squirrels frolicked among the mature oak and maple trees in the front yard.

It was the type of home that was built for a family. Hell, there was even a white picket fence that extended from the front of the house around to the back yard. Kids played in the neighbor's yard, their peals of laughter somehow managing to fray the remainder of Seven's already-jangled nerves.

Lucas laid a hand on her knee, halting its incessant bounce. "What's wrong?"

"I don't belong here," she blurted.

His brow furrowed. "Why would you say that?"

A harsh laugh bubbled up out of her throat. "The kids, the fence, the squirrels…" she paused, shaking her head. "It's a place for families. "I'm..."

Violent. Hard. A killer.

Broken.

He tightened his grip on her knee, which pulled her attention back to him.

"Hey," he began, "you belong here just as much as anyone else."

She shot a disbelieving look out the window at the kids playing next door before shifting her incredulous gaze back to his.

"Fine. Don't believe me? Well, how's this?" He pointed to his neighbor's house on the right. "The guy who lives in that house? Arrested three times for drunk driving last year. Can't hold down a job because of it. About a month ago, I disabled his car to keep him from going out for more liquor after he'd downed an entire bottle of Cuervo and a handful of Oxy."

He pointed to his neighbor's house on the left. "The lady that lives there? She's been banging her husband's best friend and business partner for about a month now. The business partner has several mob connections, best I can tell."

"There's a guy two streets over," he went on, "who lost his job as a gym teacher at the high school when the principal found out the guy'd been fucking one of his students for over a year. One of his *fifteen-year-old* students. And I'm not even mentioning the neighbors in this place I suspect of being thieves, con artists, and cheaters."

He splayed a hand over his chest. "And me? The official story is that I quit the VCU. That's true, but what no one else knows is that if I'd stayed, I would've been transferred to a desk job. My last case? Let's just say I didn't use my *charm* to get the guy to confess to kidnapping and murder."

Lucas grabbed her hand and gave her fingers a squeeze. "I have my past, you have yours. And everyone out there is generally too concerned with their own pasts to give a shit about yours. You deserve to be here every bit as much as I do, or as much as any of them do. Remember that. No one is perfect."

Seven glanced down at her hand, which looked so small in his. She was so floored—and touched, if she was being totally honest—by his concern for her feelings and sincerity that she had no idea how she should respond. So, she spewed the first thought that popped into her mind.

"Did you know it was such a dangerous neighborhood when you moved in?"

His wide answering smile revealed a dimple in his cheek she'd never noticed. Completely inexplicably, she wanted to lick that dimple.

Yep. Her edge was gone.

Damn it.

Seven's eyes widened as she stepped into the house. Lucas hoped she wasn't getting spooked again. He glanced around, trying to see the place from her perspective to determine if it was more or less threatening to her peace of mind than the outside had been.

The bright, wide, tiled foyer led to a huge open-concept space with a cozy living room at one end, and a bar-height dining room table at the other. The living room featured warm oak floors, cathedral ceilings with several skylights, and a floor-to-ceiling river rock fireplace. The walls were painted a warm buttery yellow, and his beat-to-hell brown leather conversational faced the fireplace, which had a 60" plasma television mounted above a driftwood mantel. Six-panel doors flanked the living space, four of which led to bedrooms, one to the guest bathroom.

He didn't have pictures on the walls or cozy throw blankets tossed over the furniture, and his refrigerator was never stocked with anything but the previous days' leftovers and a few outdated condiments. In other words, there really wasn't anything in his house that screamed "family." Hopefully she'd be able to relax here a little bit.

Lucas pointed to the room to the left of the foyer. "That's the master. You can stay in there."

She frowned. "Why would I take your bedroom?"

"Because the bathroom that the two guest rooms share hasn't been remodeled yet, and the shower is only pumping out cold water at the moment."

He didn't add that with her in the house, cold showers were probably just what he needed, so having him take the guest room was most likely in everyone's best interest.

Seven wandered into the living room, looking around distractedly. "Oh, I don't shower, so I can take the guest bath. There's no need to give up your room."

Wait…what? "What do you mean you don't shower?"

"I wash up in the sink, so I won't need a shower."

How in the name of all that's holy did she get all that hair washed in a sink? And why even try?

Before he could ask her any questions, Seven's attention was drawn to the lumbering beast that was suddenly hobbling toward them.

Lucas sighed. The dog had come out of the guest room. Again.

He'd paid a small fortune for the special, orthopedic dog cot the vet recommended, and this motherfucker refused to get anywhere near it. He did, however, have great affinity for the new memory foam mattress in the guest room.

He glared down at the animal. "You bastard, you were on the bed again, weren't you?"

The dog just looked up at him, completely unrepentant, and wagged his tail. His tongue lolled out the side of his mouth as he offered Lucas a doggy grin.

Seven's head tipped to one side as she studied him. "What…"

Yeah, *what is that* was a question Lucas had heard a time or two about the damn dog. "He's a pit bull. A few months ago, we busted a vampire who was running a dog-fighting ring. The other dogs were all adopted out at the pound, but they couldn't find a home for Lucky here, so I took him."

She glanced up at him, a smirk on her perfect lips. "Lucky?"

Yeah, he'd heard *that* question a time or two as well. Lucky was missing an eye and most of one front leg, was covered in various silvery scars, and had been so mangy and underfed that the vet wasn't sure he'd make it. But with proper medical attention, plenty of high-protein, expensive-as-shit dog food, and apparently, access to a memory foam mattress, Lucky had rallied like a boss.

Now, his blue-gray coat gleamed and his pale blue eyes—well, eye, he supposed—were no longer dulled with pain and hunger. And now that he'd filled out, Lucky was a lean, muscular, hundred-pound, shedding-all-over-the-bed, six-cups-of-dog-food-a-day-eating fool.

He shrugged in response to Seven's question. "He's alive, isn't he? I'd say that's lucky, given what he's been through."

She graced him with another quick smile—yeah, he was definitely going to need a cold shower if she kept doing that—before dropping down to her knees and extending her hand, palm down, to the dog, who was sitting a few feet away from her, staring her down in full-on watchdog mode.

"Hello, Lucky," she said. "I'm Seven."

"He probably won't come to you," Lucas warned. "He's pretty leery of new people."

In fact, Lucky was so leery of new people that barely anyone even knew Lucas had a dog. And honestly, after everything the poor animal had seen of human and vampire nature, who could blame him?

But that wasn't to say Lucky was scared of people. No, far from it, really. Lucas was pretty sure the mailman would never come back after Lucky barked and snarled at him through the glass on the front door. Poor guy had been so startled he'd fallen down the front steps, jumped up, and hightailed it back to his vehicle at a pretty impressive clip.

So, if he was being totally honest with himself, Lucas wasn't sure if Lucky was more likely to attack Seven, or simply keep his distance. He was unpredictable like that.

Lucas had avoided shifting into wolf form and establishing canine dominance over Lucky so far. He'd been through so much that he felt like the poor guy should be allowed to be the alpha dog for a while if it made him feel better.

But if he went after Seven, all bets were off.

Lucky moved toward her slowly, muscles tensed, looking ready to engage his fight-or-flight options at any moment. She kept her hand outstretched, giving the dog an opportunity to smell her and see if she was someone worth approaching.

Lucas released the breath he'd been holding when Lucky gingerly sniffed Seven's hand. He then must've decided she was worthy of further inspection, because he ducked under her hand so that her palm rested on top of his head.

Seven smiled and obliged his not-so-subtle request by rubbing the top his head, then behind his ears. Lucky groaned in ecstasy.

"I'll be damned," Lucas muttered as Lucky invaded Seven's space, laying his chin on her shoulder in the equivalent of a dog hug.

She laughed and wrapped her arms around Lucky's thick neck. "I guess it's a good thing we practiced hugging earlier, huh?"

He rubbed the back of his neck, doing his damnedest to pretend her laugh wasn't the sexiest thing he'd ever heard in his life. "Yeah," he said eventually. "Who could've known you'd need to use your newly acquired skills so fast?"

Watching Seven lavish attention on Lucky—and watching Lucky drop to the floor, shamelessly begging for a belly rub—Lucas realized two new things about Seven.

First, although she clearly disliked herself for things she'd done in the past, babies and dogs—who were stellar judges of character, in Lucas's experience—loved her and immediately felt comfortable with her. That said a lot about her nature, and confirmed what Lucas had known all along. Seven wasn't dangerous, and she wasn't crazy.

And secondly, every new thing he discovered about Seven only made him want to learn more. He wanted to know *her*. Not the cool exterior she so often showed to the world, but the *real* her. And more than anything, he wanted to make her smile and laugh, again and again.

So, he was developing a slight obsession with the sister of the man who married the woman Lucas *thought* he'd been in love with. And that wasn't even taking into account the fact that he'd broken her out of a mental hospital earlier that day.

When exactly, he wondered, had his life become the subject of a bad telenovela?

CHAPTER ELEVEN

One month later

The ginormous Kodiak bear that a moment ago had been Owen McCaffrey tipped its head back and roared.

Harper and Seven were standing close enough to him that the force of his breath blew their hair back and misted their faces with beer-scented bear spit.

Harper groaned and lifted the hem of her T-shirt to wipe her face. "All right, Owen, I'm losing my patience. Will you just shift back so we can talk about this like rational people?"

He curled his lip back and swiped at her with his giant paw. She leapt back in time to save her skin, but not her T-shirt.

Seven sucked in a sharp breath. Having spent the past month with Harper learning how to skip-trace bail-jumping vampires and shifters, she was starting to understand how her sister-in-law's mind worked. And Seven happened to know for a fact that the T-shirt Owen just ruined was Harper's favorite. The black *Game of Thrones* T-shirt had been a gift from Mischa, and it had *Khaleesi* spelled out in heart-shaped rhinestones across her chest. It now had three jagged claw marks over her belly button.

Now Harper was going to be pissed.

Harper snarled at him. "Owen, I'm giving you one more chance to shift and come quietly with me to the police station. Then, I'm kicking your hairy ass into next week."

He stood up on his back legs, towering over them, and roared again.

Harper glanced over at her. "If you were here by yourself, what would you do?"

"Break both his legs," Seven said without hesitation. "Hogtie him when he falls."

"Weeelll," Harper answered, hesitating, "that would definitely work. But maybe we could try something a little less violent first."

Seven kept her mouth shut. Breaking his legs *had* been her less violent idea. Harper *really* wouldn't have liked Plan A.

"All right, Owen," Harper said. "Just remember, I gave you a chance to do this the easy way."

And with that, she pulled a can of bear repellant out of her purse and sprayed him full in the face.

After a moment of furious screeching and clawing at its face, the bear slowly began to shift. Seven winced at the sound his bones made as they snapped, crackled, and popped back into the shape of a human. Was it this brutal when Lucas shifted? She hated to think of him going through that. It had to be painful.

Only when a naked—and marginally less hairy—Owen laid at their feet did Harper let Seven truss him up with a set of zip ties, one around his wrists and one around his ankles.

"Fuck, Harper," he whined. "You didn't have to use that shit on me."

"Owen, this is the third time you've broken your bond agreement and failed to appear in court. I have *no* idea how you keep convincing Big Bill to post for you, but I'm sick of skip- tracing your ass and you swiping at me for my trouble."

"I'm sorry, Harper. I just can't go back to jail," he said, sticking his lower lip out in a pitiful pout.

To an outside observer, it would probably look like Harper was being a big bully. In his human form, Owen was beyond pathetic. About five-six, one-thirty with an overbite and an unruly mop of dirty blond hair, he looked like a guy who'd been down on his luck his entire life. But Harper knew this particularly luckless loser was a deadbeat dad, and she had no patience for that.

And Seven couldn't help but notice that while he was telling the courts he didn't have any money, he was here, at a bar, dropping money on bad hand after bad hand of poker with other local scumbags. Short of that, he could be found at the Kitty Kat Palace, slipping ones into Misty Mountain's G-string.

Seven tightened his bindings until he yelped. He started to protest, but she shut him down with a sharp look that had him swallowing hard and averting his eyes.

Harper rolled her eyes at him. "You can quit your whining and put the sad puppy dog eyes away, Owen. I'm not ever going to feel sorry for you. Just pay your child support, loser."

"Aw, come on, Harper. We all make mistakes. It's not like you two are so perfect, either. Everyone knows you both worked for Sentry." His eyes cut to Seven briefly, then back to Harper. "And everyone knows what *she* did there. You know what they're calling her on the streets? The Angel of Death."

Violet had warned her that the Midvale guards were running their mouths, and that the paranormal community was small and prone to gossip.

Don't let it break you down. You can't change your past, but you can control your actions from this point on. Be the person you want to be. Don't let yourself be defined by the past.

She could practically recite Violet's words on auto-pilot, she'd heard them so much.

Lucas usually gave her his own variation of the speech. It went something like, *you're the only one who can make you feel like shit. Don't listen to those stupid motherfuckers. They're just trying to break you so they can feel better about their own pathetic lives.*

Less inspirational than Vi's version? Possibly. But no less powerful.

Deciding to take their advice, Seven shrugged off Owen's comments. But there was still a tiny little part of her that wished she'd broken his legs when she'd had the chance.

Harper snorted. "Nice try, Owen, but we're not going to suddenly realize we're kindred loser spirits and let you go. You're going to the station as soon as I find a blanket for you to sit on, because there's no *way* I'm letting your bare ass touch the leather upholstery in my car."

Owen sighed and rolled to a sitting position. "Well, thanks for not sending Riddick after me this time, at least."

"What makes you think she didn't?"

Owen's eyes widened at the raspy growl that came out of nowhere. Harper grinned as Riddick melted out of the shadows.

Riddick sighted Harper down like prey and stalked over to her. When he was close enough that she had to tip her head back to meet his eyes, he gave her a gentle shove back against the wall, then proceeded to kiss her silly. When he stepped back, she licked her lips and gave him a breathless, "Hi."

Seven felt a pang of want in her gut. In her Sentry days, she'd never been in a position to want the kind of relationship Harper had with Riddick. But now? She found she was increasingly envious of what they shared, and not just the emotional connection. She was equally jealous of all the sex they were obviously having.

Seven had only had the occasion to have sex once with a fellow Sentry cleaner. There'd been no emotion involved, but the physical act itself had been very…satisfying. Definitely something she wouldn't mind repeating. Soon.

Riddick grinned down at Harper, before turning to Seven. "How're you doing, sweetheart?"

He'd been calling her that for the past couple of weeks. It still always took her a moment before she realized she was *sweetheart* to him. "I'm fine."

"Why didn't you wait for me?" he asked Harper. "I told you I'd go after this jackass as soon as I got done with Mrs. Perrigrino's husband."

"Find anything?" Harper asked.

Riddick nodded, looking grim, and Seven's stomach fell.

Mrs. Perrigrino was a little old lady who hit the lottery after playing the same numbers every week for thirty years. Shortly thereafter, she met a disarmingly handsome, sophisticated vampire, fell in love at first sight, and got married.

Mrs. Perrigrino's adult kids hired Harper Hall Investigations to find out if the vampire had married their mother for her money. Riddick had been tailing the vamp for a week and had apparently found the evidence the kids expected.

Poor Mrs. Perrigrino.

Harper shook her head, looking sad, and said, "Mrs. Perrigrino was more important. I knew Seven and I could take care of Yogi here by ourselves."

"Getting kind of sick of being called names," Owen grumbled.

"Shut up," Harper and Riddick said in stereo while Seven barely resisted the urge to kick him in the shins.

"Who has Haven?" Riddick asked.

"My mom," Harper said, then frowned. "She snatched that child out of my arms like she hadn't seen her in a freakin' year or something, then practically shoved me out the door. I'm a second-class citizen in that house compared to Haven."

Riddick smiled at her, but then his gaze dropped to the tear in his wife's shirt and all warmth bled from his eyes.

Seven knew this look. She'd seen it in the mirror a time or two.

Owen obviously knew the look too, because he immediately lifted his bound hands to cover his face and started trying to curl up against the wall. "Shit, man, you know I don't have much control over what I do in bear form, right? I'd never hurt her on purpose."

"He was mean to Seven, too," Harper added, not even trying to calm her husband down, sounding a little bored with the whole thing.

Riddick stalked over to Owen, looking determined and more than a little feral.

Owen whimpered. "Call him off!"

Harper snorted. "He's not a dog. I can't 'call him off'."

Riddick leaned down and plucked Owen off the ground by his bound wrists and shoved him against the wall, holding him several inches off the ground.

"I'm only going to say this once," he growled. "Never. Ever. Touch. Her. Or I will strangle you with your own intestines and laugh while I do it."

Owen looked like he might pee himself, but that didn't stop Riddick from adding, "The same goes for my sister. When you insult her, you insult me. Do you want to insult *me*, Owen?"

Owen shook his head furiously. "No. Jesus, no."

"You should apologize to us," Harper suggested, examining a split in one of her fingernails. "Especially to Seven."

"Jesus Christ, I'm so fucking sorry. Swear to *God* I am."

Harper glanced over at her. "You good with that?"

Seven quickly nodded, not entirely sure what Riddick would do if she didn't accept Owen's apology.

Harper shrugged. "Guess I am, too, then."

Riddick unclenched his fist, letting Owen drop unceremoniously to the ground.

It took Seven a moment or two to process what had just happened. Riddick had been in a murderous rage. She'd seen it. Hell, she'd *felt* it. Harper must've seen it, too, but she hadn't done anything to stop him. Quite the opposite, really. Why hadn't she intervened?

Because she knew no matter how angry he was, he was in control, Seven realized. Harper *trusted* him. Just like Lucas trusted her. Riddick was obviously worthy of Harper's trust. Maybe, just maybe, she was worthy of Lucas's trust, too.

It was a crazy thought. Humbling and terrifying and…exciting all at the same time. If she actually *was* trustworthy, if she *actually* had it in her to be a good person who contributed to society in ways other than killing, was it *possible* that she could find the kind of love Harper and Riddick shared?

Be the person you want to be.

For once, Violet's order seemed entirely…possible.

When Riddick had shoved Owen into the trunk of Harper's car (apparently his apology hadn't earned him enough favor with Riddick to warrant a ride in the back seat), Harper told her, "You know, I think we need to do another shopping trip. The clothes you picked out last time? They look good on you, but they're certainly not helping you lose your Angel of Death title."

Seven glanced down at her black leather jacket, black tank top, black cargo pants, and black Doc Martens. When she met Harper's eyes, she could see the teasing glint there. "You're probably right," she admitted.

Harper grinned at her. "We'll go soon. And next time we have to pick up Owen? Let's do things your way."

Seven blinked. "I can break his legs?"

"I think you've earned it."

Seven returned her wide smile. This whole *fitting in with a family* thing? Maybe it wasn't going to be so difficult after all. Not with *this* family, at least.

CHAPTER TWELVE

Considering they were a werewolf and a *dhampyre* living together in the suburbs (which sounded like the set up for a bad sitcom, for Christ's sake), Lucas and Seven had fallen into a very…domesticated routine over the past few weeks.

Lucas spent his days in Monroe, which was one county south of Whispering Hope. Monroe PD had been desperate enough for help that they'd taken him on immediately, without really inquiring too much about why he'd left his old department. The other guys in homicide didn't trust him just yet, which was fairly typical of any newcomer, let alone a newcomer who'd come from a vampire crimes unit—but they were mostly a decent bunch.

And dealing with human criminals was a lot more satisfying than dealing with the paranormal ones. Sometimes he was even able to help deliver *actual* justice, novel idea that it was.

Seven spent her days with her brother and Harper, learning what it took to be a paranormal private investigator. She also had therapy sessions with Vi twice a week, and spent some quality time on the side with Harper and Mischa, who were schooling her on pop culture and the importance of well-executed sarcasm.

But the evenings? Well, those belonged to Lucas and Seven. They'd get home about the same time and forage for food together, which usually ended with him ordering take out since neither of them could cook worth shit. And while they ate, they talked. There were never any lulls in their conversation, and they'd talk for hours about anything and everything. He now knew more about Seven than he suspected anyone in the world did, and vice versa.

He knew she hated vegetables but ate them because they were healthy. He knew her music preferences all fell heavily into the rock family, and when he tried to get her to listen to country or pop, she'd just shake her head and wrinkle her nose adorably.

He knew that watching *The Walking Dead* made her edgy, but that she'd snatch the remote out of his hand if he even thought about changing the channel while it was on. He knew she fed Lucky scraps off her plate when she thought he wasn't looking. He knew she was cranky in the morning until she had her coffee, which was why he made sure to wake up before her and have a fresh pot ready to go by the time she stumbled out of bed and made her way to the kitchen every morning.

He knew she almost always fell asleep every night at midnight whether she wanted to or not. And when she fell asleep next to him on the couch watching TV, he could pick her up and carry her to bed without waking her.

And more than anything, he knew he wanted to know *more* about her. He liked everything he'd learned so far, and it was getting harder and harder to friend-zone her.

He'd been living in a semi-hard state ever since she walked into his house. Her voice, the way she said his name, her perfect pink lips, the way her eyes softened when she talked about Haven, the fact that even after Harper had bought her all new clothes, she still chose to sleep in an old Whispering Hope PD T-shirt of his that she'd liberated from his closet on her first night in his house…it all turned him on. Shit, he was starting to think he was going to end up with a permanent imprint of his zipper on his dick from all the erections he was sporting in her presence.

But every time he found himself staring at her mouth and wondering what those perfect lips would taste like, he'd pull back.

When he was with Seven, he felt like a complete idiot for having ever thought Harper had been the one for him. Seven fit into his life seamlessly, and the thought of rushing her into anything and blowing what they could have before it ever really started was…well, if he was being honest with himself, it was fucking terrifying.

But, nauseating terror aside, he'd be damned if he was going to completely ignore his feelings—and what he thought she was feeling in return—for too much longer. When the time was right, preferably *very* soon, he'd…

His phone vibrated in his pocket. "Hey, Vi," he answered. "Seven's not here. Want me to have her call you back?"

"No, I called to talk to you."

Her tone didn't bode well for what he'd hoped would be another peaceful evening at home. He sighed. "What's wrong?"

Violet paused for so long he thought she might be purposefully screwing with his patience, but she eventually said, "I got the remainder of Dr. Daniels' files."

Well, shit.

"What happened to her?" he asked, completely unable to keep the angry growl out his voice.

"Oh, Lucas," she said, her voice breaking on his name. "He tortured that poor girl for *years*. Experimented on her to test her healing abilities and strength."

A haze of red descended over his vision and his wolf demanded blood.

Hunt. Trap. Shred. Kill.

"What kind of experiments?" he forced himself to ask.

"Drowning was his favorite. He did it to see how much longer she could hold her breath than a regular human and how much faster she could regain consciousness."

Hunt. Trap. Shred. Kill.

"I'll fucking kill him," he hissed.

At his feet, Lucky whimpered, and Lucas took several steadying breaths, trying to fight back his wolf, which was all but demanding to be unleashed.

Vi snorted. "You won't have to. Hunter is letting Mischa decide Daniels's punishment on behalf of the Council. He'll be begging for death by the time she gets done with him."

That was acceptable, he thought grudgingly. Not as good as squeezing the bastard's neck until his head popped off, but acceptable. "Why are you telling *me* this, Vi?"

She paused again, and he growled, "Just fucking spit it out."

"Hey," she snapped, "don't yell at me or I swear to God I'll come over there and smack you on the nose with a rolled-up newspaper again!"

His anger dimmed a fraction as he remembered her doing that very thing once before. Not his finest moment, of that he was certain.

"I'm telling you this because when we're in therapy all I hear is *Lucas this* and *Lucas that* and *Lucas says*. She's taking to her family as well as can be expected, but right now, you're her emotional center, her rock," Vi said. "I can't tell Harper and Riddick about this. Riddick will absolutely lose his shit if he ever finds out about what happened to her."

Yeah, Lucas thought wryly as he continued to wrestle with his wolf for control of his own body, *because I'm such a pillar of fucking strength over here.*

"What do you want me to do?" he asked through gritted teeth.

"I want you to be on the lookout for signs of PTSD. A human who's been through what she has would be scary enough, but someone with her strength? She could hurt someone completely unintentionally."

He took a few more steadying breaths. "Fine. What are the signs of PTSD?"

"Well, depression and hopelessness are common. Nightmares and flashbacks, too, obviously. Irritability or angry outbursts…"

So far so good, he thought. Seven didn't seem to have any of that.

"…headaches, hypervigilance…"

He scoffed at that last one. Just because she checked the locks on the doors and windows a few times before bed—after he'd already checked them—didn't necessarily mean she had PTSD. Vigilance seemed like a perfectly natural response in her situation.

"…disrupted sleep, insomnia…"

He frowned. He *did* sometimes hear her moving around her room after two or so. He just assumed she was like him and only really needed a few hours' sleep a night. He hadn't considered the possibility of insomnia, or that maybe a nightmare had awoken her.

"…and making an effort to avoid things that remind her of what happened at Midvale."

Like washing up in the sink to avoid taking a shower that might remind her of drowning.

Shit.

"I might've seen some of those signs," he mumbled.

Vi sighed. "I was afraid of that. Don't bring it up with her, OK? I'll start talking to her about this in our next session. And in the meantime…"

There it was again. That damned annoying pause that made him want to come through the phone and shake her. "Just say it, Vi."

"All right, fine. I'm just going to be blunt about this."

Well that'd be a pleasant change of pace, wouldn't it?

"I've seen the way you look at her, and I've seen the look in her eyes when she talks about you."

He blinked. That wasn't *at all* where he thought the conversation had been going. Never let it be said that Vi was boring or predictable. "And?"

She muttered something under her breath he didn't quite catch, but was pretty sure it ended with "jackass," before saying, "*And* she's not ready for any kind of…romantic relationship right now. You need to back off."

Well, that pissed him off on a couple of different levels. First and foremost, his…*whatever it was* with Seven was none of Vi's business. And secondly, did Vi have such a low opinion of him that she thought he'd pressure Seven into a relationship with him? Did she think he was *that* much of a dick?

"You should know me well enough to know I'd never hurt her," he said, indignant.

"Never intentionally," she hedged. "But you're a man, and she's an incredibly beautiful woman who's living with you—"

"So I'm automatically going to try and nail her at every opportunity? Jesus, Vi," he muttered in disgust. Then an ugly thought occurred to him. "Are you sure this is even about her? Is this about what happened with us?"

"Don't flatter yourself," she shot back sharply. "I'm most definitely not pining for you and working to romantically sabotage you, you dick. In fact, I have a date tonight, so rest assured that I have moved past our little…flirtation, for lack of a better word."

If he hadn't already been up for the title of world's biggest asshole, he could now be assured he had it in the bag.

"I'm really sorry, Vi. That was a shitty thing to accuse you of." He raked a hand through his hair. "This whole thing with Seven, it's just…"

She sighed again as he trailed off. "I know all of this is overwhelming. But if *you're* overwhelmed, think about how she must be feeling. PTSD is no joke, Lucas. Give her the time and space she needs to heal."

He offered Vi another heartfelt apology and assured her he'd heard everything she said before he disconnected the call.

Well, hell. What was he supposed to do now? He was living with a woman he wanted so bad it was nearly painful, he was pretty sure she wanted him too, and he couldn't do a damn thing about it for fear of triggering her PTSD from something that never should've happened to her in the first place. What a clusterfuck.

Lucky began to do an all-over body wag that Lucas had come to understand meant Seven was home. The dog made his way to the door to greet her faster than any three-legged dog had a right to move.

She came through the door and immediately dropped to her knees and opened her arms to Lucky, who was positively quivering with joy as he whined happily and frantically licked her face. She laughed as she stood up and wiped her face on her sleeve.

"I'm happy to see you, too, buddy," Seven said as she gave him one last pat on the head.

Lucas felt gut-punched as her eyes met his and her smile grew. Goddamn, was he ever going to get used to the power of that smile?

"Hi," she said, somewhat breathlessly. "Did you still want to watch a movie tonight?"

The hopeful note in her voice was impossible to miss, and once again, he felt like the world's biggest asshole, because he knew he just wasn't capable of sitting next to her on the couch tonight—breathing in the scent of her skin, listening to her sweet voice, seeing her smile—and not touching her. Especially after what he'd learned today. He just wasn't strong enough.

He cleared his throat. "Uh, no. Sorry. I…have to go back to the station. Got some paperwork to finish up."

The smile bled from her face slowly and Lucas wanted to howl at the loss of it. And for being the cause of it.

"That was a lie," she said quietly. "Why did you lie to me?"

And why couldn't he seem to remember she was more accurate than a fucking lie detector? "Shit," he blurted out, causing her to flinch. "I'm sorry," he quickly added. "I just need…*we* just need some space. That's all."

A frown line popped up between her brows. "You want…space from me?"

God no. There was way too much space between them as it was. "I didn't say *want*. I said *need*. It would be best if we got some space."

Jesus, he sounded like a fucking tool. But there was no way around it. Vi was right. Seven was too busy dealing with her own emotions to deal with his. It wasn't fair of him to ask anything of her right now.

After a moment of intense study in which he was pretty sure she was staring directly into his brain, she nodded. "I understand what you're saying."

Really? 'Cause he sure as fuck didn't. "Good. That's good."

"I'll just go…" she trailed off, pointing to her room.

"Yeah, sure. Fine," he said, like an idiot.

A moment after she'd gone, Lucky shot him a look of what could only be described as disgust and disappointment. Until that moment, he hadn't even known dogs were *capable* of looking down on someone. If the look hadn't been directed at him, Lucas would've been impressed.

Lucas gave him a palms-up what-the-hell gesture. "Well, what the fuck was I supposed to do?"

Lucky huffed out a breath and wandered away, pawing at Seven's door until she let him in. Neither of them looked back at him before she shut the door again.

So, all in the course of five minutes, he'd hurt Seven, most likely managed to ruin whatever budding relationship they'd had, *and* lost an argument with his dog.

Good going, asshole. Super smooth.

Shaking his head in disgust at himself, he grabbed his jacket and got the fuck out of the house before he did something stupid.

Well, stupid*er*, he supposed.

CHAPTER THIRTEEN

"Aw, dude, the way you flipped that shifter to the ground and put your foot down on his nads when he tried to get up? That was *classic*. Harper's gonna be pissed she missed it."

Benny laughed until he snorted and slumped over on the bar, clutching his side.

Seven didn't understand what was so funny. Harper told them to apprehend the shifter who'd failed to show up for his hearing. She'd done that. She hadn't even broken his legs.

"A man's testicles are very sensitive," she said in her own defense. "It was an effective way to keep him on the ground until you could tie him up."

He snorted again and swiped at his watering eyes with the back of his hand. "Yeah, babe, it was *highly* effective. I'm not sure I've ever seen a shifter's eyes bug out like that."

He paused and mimicked the shifter's expression, cracking himself up again in the process. When the snort-laughs died down to mere chuckles, he added, "I thought I was gonna piss myself, I was laughing so fucking hard. That settles it, though." He banged his palm down on the bar. "I'm telling Harper I refuse to do skip-tracing without you from now on. That was the best time I've had all month."

He held up his shot glass of tequila and clinked it against her water glass.

"So, you…like working with me?" she asked, still somewhat confused.

"Abso-fuckin'-lutely!" he answered with a wide grin. "That's why I invited you here—to my home away from home—to celebrate the beginning of a beautiful friendship."

Well, she thought, glancing around the dingy bar, his *home away from home* wasn't that impressive, but given her level of social awkwardness, she probably couldn't afford to turn away an offer of friendship.

"And hey," he went on, "I'm real sorry about the day we met. You know, when I implied you was a sociopath? I didn't mean nothin' by it. You're good people, Seven. Just like Lucas said."

Her stomach sank at the mention of Lucas. He'd been avoiding her for over a week. She still had no idea what she'd done wrong. One day, he seemed like he wanted to spend time with her, and the next, he couldn't seem to get away fast enough.

And the absolute worst part of his rejection? She couldn't even get mad at him about it. She was too hurt to get angry. Anger was an easy emotion. All you had to do was hit something and yell and rage, and the anger fled almost as soon as it came. But hurt? It was new to her, and she had absolutely no clue what to do with it.

Benny snapped his fingers in front of her face. "What happened there, doll? I lost ya for a second. You OK?"

"I'm fine," she lied.

"Pfffttt. No, you're not. And you're a shitty liar, too." He nudged her with his shoulder. "Come on. Tell your good buddy Benny what's wrong. Maybe I can help."

Seven swiveled on her barstool so that she was facing him. Maybe he was right. "I've never had a friend before. Does talking to a friend help you when you're feeling hurt about something?"

"Oh, yeah," he answered immediately. "I always feel better about shit when I talk it through with Harper and Riddick and Mischa."

"Well," he amended, "in all fairness, I'm not sure Riddick considers me a *friend.* But he hasn't tried to burn me alive lately, so there's *that.*"

She'd have to file that bit of information away for later. Too confusing. She gave her head a shake before saying, "So, you're my friend?"

"Yeah, babe. What's up?"

"Am I someone you'd be interested in having sex with?"

Benny spit the mouthful of tequila he'd just swallowed directly in the bartender's face.

"Fucking hell, Benny," he said, wiping his face with the dirty bar rag he kept tucked into the waistband of his pants.

"Sorry, Tiny," Benny choked.

Tiny grumbled something Seven didn't quite understand before wandering away. She watched Benny expectantly while he coughed and looked at her like she'd sprouted a second head. The expression of horror and shock on his face was most likely answer enough to her question, but she decided to hear what he had to say anyway. That was what a friend would do, she thought.

But what the hell did she know about friends?

“Babe,” Benny said after the world’s longest pause, “I’m sure I didn’t hear you right. Did you…ask me…Jesus, I can’t even say it out loud it’s so crazy.”

Seven shrugged, tracing her fingertips through the wet ring her glass had left on the scarred oak bar. “I see Harper with Riddick and I wonder if anyone could…want *me*. You know, like that. That’s what I was asking. Would you ever want me like that?”

His eyes went wide. “Shit, no, I wouldn’t.”

So, here’s embarrassment again, she thought. Yep. It was every bit as distasteful as it’d been the first time she felt it. “OK. I understand. Thank you for being honest with me.”

He grabbed her hand when she tried to stand up. “No, no, no. You don’t get it at all. There’s three very good reasons why I could never want you like that. Number one, Riddick would kill me. I mean, we’re talking peel-my-skin-like-an-orange-and-stake-me-out-to-greet-the-fucking-dawn *dead*.”

He shuddered. “Secondly, you are so far outta my league…it’d take the *light* of your league, like, a gazillion years to even shine on my sorry ass.”

She frowned. “What do you mean?”

“You’re…” he gestured to her face and body, “…all *this*, and I’m...” he gestured to his own face and body, “…*this*. You could do better. *Way* better. You're a ten and I'm a two. Tens stick with tens and twos stick with twos."

She gave that information a moment to process before commenting, "That seems really shallow. And probably inaccurate. I heard that woman at the coffee stand outside Harper's building say you were a total…*hottie*, I think she said. That must mean you're at least a seven, right?"

He blinked. "Shit, really? Coffee-stand Celia thinks I'm hot? When was…" he trailed off, shaking his head. "That's not the point. We was talkin' about you."

Seven nodded. "What's the third reason?"

"That's easy. Lucas is over the fucking moon for you, and I'd never cock-block him. He's a good dude. A little scary sometimes, but a good dude nonetheless. Bros before hoes and all that."

His eyes went wide again. "Not that you're a ho. Jesus, don't step on my nads or tell Riddick I said that, OK?"

She waved off his concern, much more interested in what he'd said about Lucas. "Do you really think Lucas likes me?"

Benny snorted. "Shit, *like* you? The way he looks at you? I ain't never seen him look at anyone like that."

Hope bloomed in her chest. Maybe they had a chance after all.

"Well," Benny went on, "except for Harper, of course."

Funny thing about hope. Seemed it could wither and die just as quickly as it bloomed.

"Lucas is in love with Harper," she said, her voice sounding dull even to her own ears. It wasn't a question. She'd known he was lying to her about something related to Harper. She'd just been too naïve to figure it out.

"No," Benny said quickly. "I don't think he is any…shit, are you OK? You look kinda…"

Murderously angry? Yep. That'd explain her increased blood pressure and respirations. And the fact that her face felt ready to go up in flames, right up to the tips of her ears.

He wanted space, huh? Space to figure out how to steal Harper from her brother? And if that failed, was she supposed to wait around and be his consolation prize?

Fuck that.

Fuck *him.*

"I want to do another skip-trace," she said through clenched teeth.

Benny swallowed hard. "There aren't any more. We got 'em all."

He let out a squeak when she grabbed the front of his shirt and lifted him right off his bar stool.

"I. Need. To. Hit. Something. Now."

Benny looked nervous for a minute, then a grin—a totally evil grin—spread across his face. "I got just the thing, doll."

CHAPTER FOURTEEN

The way you knew you were doing the right thing was if it made you feel like complete shit.

At least, that was Lucas's recent experience with doing the right thing.

It had been three weeks since Vi gave him her little stay-away-from-Seven-for-her-own-good speech, and he found he was getting progressively more dickish (Harper's word, not his) every day.

And Seven…

He sighed. Seven had seemed to shift from hurt to good and pissed off with admirable speed. He guessed he should be thankful. Seeing her hurt had damn near killed him. Her anger wasn't any fun, but he could deal with it.

Mostly he could deal with it because their conversations had been reduced to gestures. He said hello, she grunted in reply, then stomped off and slammed a door.

He'd come to think of the slammed door as a middle finger held high.

Not that he blamed her. The graceless way he'd demanded space was probably more worthy of a kick to the balls than it was an implied digital fuck-you. She was taking the high road in his opinion.

What he really needed was a good case to distract himself with, but sadly, the crime rate in Monroe was practically nil at the moment. He'd been working so hard to stay away from home that he'd managed to clean up the bulk of their current case load and all their cold cases in the past few weeks. Now the place was like fucking Mayberry. He wouldn't be surprised if Aunt Bee strolled into the station at any minute with a pie.

But it wasn't Aunt Bee who strolled into the station right about then.

Noah Riddick strolled in like he owned the place. Well, *stalked* was probably a better word for it. The guy was way too intense to ever do anything as laid back as *strolling*. His narrowed eyes scanned the bullpen until they landed on Lucas.

Every cop in the building immediately went on high alert. Six-two, about two hundred pounds of lean muscle, wearing a black leather jacket and a don't-fuck-with-me expression, Riddick probably looked like a drug lord or gun runner to these guys.

"Always a pleasure to see you, Riddick," Lucas said with absolutely zero sincerity as the monosyllabic douchebag stopped in front of his desk. He jerked his head in the direction of what looked to be blood splatter on the front of Riddick's T-shirt. "Cut yourself shaving?"

He glanced down distractedly. "Broken nose."

And...Riddick's nose looked fine. That was rather telling. Probably work-related. And knowing any more than that about Harper's business was bound to irk the shit out of him, so he let it go. "To what do I owe the honor?"

Riddick's fists clenched and unclenched at his sides, and the look of pure contempt and disgust in his eyes reminded him distinctly of the way Seven looked at him lately.

Seemed he couldn't do anything right by the Riddick family these days.

"What the fuck did you do to my sister?" Riddick growled.

Lucas sat up straighter. "What's wrong? Is she OK? Where is she?"

Riddick waved off his concern. "She's with Harper at the office. She's safe. She's just not…happy."

Thanks for the news flash, Ace.

Like all the slammed doors and her look of death hadn't clued him in on her displeasure. "So, why are you here?"

"Because it's your fault she's unhappy."

"Did she say that?"

His expression went flat. "Yeah, we had a long talk about each other's feelings, hugged it out, then braided each other's hair."

Touché. Score one for the douchebag. "Yeah, OK, I get it. She's not a talker. No idea where she might have picked up a trait like that. So, if she's not talking, what makes you think this is my fault?"

Riddick raked his hands through his hair. "Look, I ask her if she's OK, and she says, 'I'm fine.' I've been married long enough to know that when a woman says she's fine, she means the opposite. So then I ask her if everything is OK at your place—because you know I would be overjoyed to pull her the fuck out of there and beat the shit of you—and her face gets all…scrunchy."

Lucas lifted a brow. "Scrunchy?"

"Yeah. Scrunchy. It's the same look Haven gets when I put her down for a nap and she's not tired, OK? Scrunchy."

Riddick looked beyond exasperated, and under any other circumstances, Lucas would've enjoyed the hell out of it. But under these circumstances? He kind of felt sorry for the guy. If the roles were reversed, he'd want to beat the shit out of the guy who made his sister unhappy, too.

Lucas sighed. "Look, I didn't do anything to her. Vi thought maybe it would be a good thing if we didn't get too…attached to one another. So, I told her we needed some space."

The pause on Riddick's end was so long Lucas thought maybe the conversation was over. But then Riddick did something Lucas had only ever seen him do in Harper's presence.

He smiled.

"Well, shit," Riddick eventually said, maintaining his huge, irritating-as-fuck grin, "I guess there's no need to worry about her wanting anything to do with *you* anytime soon. Especially since you just told her she was clingy and pathetic."

"I never said that," he said with a frown.

"No, you didn't *mean* to say that," Riddick corrected. "But that's what she heard."

Lucas scoffed. "Fuck, man, you been watching Nicholas Sparks movies or what? You sound like a damn girl."

"Yeah, 'cause mentioning Nicholas Sparks makes you sound real fucking manly."

Lucas suddenly really missed the days when Riddick barely spoke. "I have work to do, you know."

Riddick glanced around at the gaping cops disdainfully. "I can tell. Looks crazy around here."

Score two *for the douchebag.* "Wrap it up, Riddick," he grumbled. "I'm losing patience."

Riddick looked like he couldn't possibly care any less about Lucas's patience. "The whole 'space' speech definitely explains her scrunchy face, but not why she's been hanging out with Benny every night and came to work today with a cut on her cheek."

Lucas shot to his feet. "Bury the lead, why don't you, asshole! Someone hurt her?"

He shrugged. "I don't know. Maybe. She said she fell."

"Did you ask Benny what's going on?"

Riddick's glance labeled Lucas as the dumbest motherfucker on the planet. "No. Why ask a guy I work with every day when I can come down here—way, way out of my way to talk with someone I can't stand who makes my sister's face scrunchy?"

Jesus, apparently Harper's supreme command of sarcasm was rubbing off on her husband. "So, you're saying Benny backed the 'I fell' story?"

"Yep. I was going to call Tina in to talk to him, but…" he trailed off and shrugged again.

But Tina was terrifying and no one wanted to have to call her unless it was their absolute last resort, Lucas mentally finished the rest of Riddick's statement. If *Lucas* was terrified of her, he couldn't imagine what it was like for Riddick to have her as a mother-in-law.

"I'll talk to Benny," Lucas said. And by "talk," he meant hang the little prick out a ten-story window by his feet until he spilled his guts.

"Good. Straighten this shit out, Cooper. I don't want to have to kill you."

And with that, Riddick turned on his heel and walked away.

"Nice chatting with you, as always," Lucas called out to his retreating back.

Riddick didn't bother looking back or slowing his steps, just lifted his middle finger high as he marched right out the door. Every cop in the building let out a collective sigh of relief when he was gone.

Charming dude. No wonder Harper's so crazy about him.

Which made him wonder…

Swiping his phone off the desk, he punched in Harper's number. He didn't bother with a greeting when she answered, just asked, "Hypothetically, if I told you we needed space, what would you think I meant by that?"

"Oh, Jesus," she grumbled after a short pause. "Tell me you did *not* say that to Seven. Is that why her face gets all scrunchy when anyone mentions you?"

Lucas pinched the bridge of his nose and closed his eyes. Son of a bitch, he hated it when Riddick was right.

When he didn't answer, she let out an exasperated sigh. "You moron! You better fix this, Lucas. I'd hate to have to ask Riddick to kill you."

No worries there. If he wasn't able to set things straight with Seven, she'd probably kill him in his sleep before too long.

"So much for doing the right thing," he muttered after Harper hung up on him.

CHAPTER FIFTEEN

Benny didn't even notice Lucas had been tailing him for the past ten blocks. Hopefully Harper only used the guy for skip- tracing, because any detective worth his salt would've noticed a tail by now.

Lucas sat in his truck and watched from across the street as Benny crawled through a gaping hole in the chain-link fence that surrounded the old foundry.

"What the hell are you doing, Benny?" he muttered to himself.

As a former member of the VCU, Lucas knew what went on in this old abandoned building. Of course, with 90% of the force on the take, no one bothered to shut down the illegal gambling and fighting that went on inside. Besides, why should good folk—good *human* folk, that is—care about a bunch of vamps consensually beating the shit out of each?

The Vampire Council usually kept its distance, too, only getting involved if and when someone died. Hunter and his predecessors felt that if the paranormals were taking their aggressions out on each other in a controlled setting away from the rest of society, all was well.

On a typical day, Lucas didn't give a shit either.

But today wasn't a typical day.

Harper said she'd heard Benny tell Seven he'd meet her around 9:30 or so. It was 9:45, and since he hadn't seen hide nor hair of her, Lucas had to assume Seven was already inside, which pissed him off to no end.

What the hell was Benny thinking? Bringing Seven to a shithole like this to watch vamps beat the fuck out of each other was bad enough, but leaving her *alone* in there? Jesus, he didn't even want to *think* about all the bad shit that could've gone down.

Yeah, he wasn't exactly sure Benny was going to come out of this alive, he thought as he entered the building in Benny's tracks.

The inside of the shithole was even worse than the outside, and the outside looked like a bombed-out hovel in Beirut.

The place was wall-to-wall crumbling concrete, stained with God knows what kinds of mold and filth and bodily fluids. The air was thick with the scent of sweat, blood, and testosterone. Graffiti—not the artistic kind, but the kind that got kids arrested for defacing property—covered just about every flat surface.

And the place was packed, filled to capacity with bloodthirsty idiots who were baying and howling like a pack of junkyard dogs. They were going nuts, jumping and punching the air as two guys in a giant cage in the center of the place pounded the hell out of each other.

He lost count of the number of times he was tempted to get his badge and gun from the car and clear the place as he elbowed and shoved his way through the crowd to the cage. As he suspected, Benny was right up front in the thick of the action, grinning like a maniac and collecting money as he took bets on the action in the cage.

Lucas didn't bother with a greeting. He just grabbed Benny by the throat, lifted him off the ground, and shoved his back against the cage.

"Where is she?" Lucas snarled.

Benny knew better than to struggle. He was half Lucas's size, and on his best day, wasn't nearly as strong as Lucas on his worst. "She's safe, man," he choked out. "I swear to God she's safe."

Right. In a room full of pumped-up jackasses screaming for blood, she was safe. And he was the fucking Easter Bunny. Even a *dhampyre* could get into trouble in a pit like this. "We'll talk about why you brought her here later," he said through clenched teeth. "But for now, we just need to get her the fuck out of here."

"That might be a problem," Benny said, gasping as Lucas tightened his grip.

"Why?"

The crackling of the PA system interrupted whatever Benny was going to say.

"You wanted it, and you're going to get it, folks," the announcer said, his voice booming through the overhead speakers. "Our undefeated champ is here tonight, and this time, the fight's personal. Ivan's back, all healed up after the last beating he took, and he wants the title that was stolen from him."

Lucas blinked. Could he be talking about Ivan Costanov? The big Russian vamp from Sayersville? Shit, someone took that giant down?

Ivan was six-foot-eight inches and 400 pounds of solid muscle. He'd been an amateur boxer full of promise—undefeated—before he'd died in a freak car wreck and been turned into a vampire by his then-manager. As a human, he'd been absolutely brutal, merciless. Every one of his victories had been by early knockout.

Lucas had followed the guy's career and often wondered what he was up to now, since there was no official vampire boxing league. Guess this answered his question.

Benny started to squirm. "Let me explain, man…"

"And here she is," the announcer shouted over the crowd. "Your champion: The Angel of Death!"

The roar of the crowd was almost deafening as Lucas shifted his gaze from the announcer back to Benny, who smiled weakly at him.

"I don't guess you'd consider not killing me if I gave you my cut of her winnings, would you?" Benny asked hopefully.

Lucas dropped him to the ground and looked into the cage to see Seven—looking so, so tiny and heart-wrenchingly beautiful in her black tank top, black cargo pants, and steel-toed work boots—standing toe-to-toe with Ivan, who towered over her so much it would've been comical if it didn't scare the shit out of him.

She looked completely at ease, nearly expressionless. Ivan, on the other hand, had blood in his eyes. He wanted to tear her apart and she looked like she couldn't care less.

"No chance, Benny," he muttered.

Benny sighed. "Yeah, that's what I thought you'd say."

CHAPTER SIXTEEN

It made no sense at all to Seven that Ivan would return to the cage. She'd beaten him in under a minute the last time. It wasn't as if he'd gotten any faster or stronger since then.

Although, he'd definitely do better this time. Benny had told her the crowd was disappointed with quick victories. They liked to see a more drawn-out battle. More hits, more tricks, more bloodshed.

Yet another aspect of human behavior that was absolutely foreign to Seven.

But at this point, she didn't really care. Being in the cage gave her the one thing she needed most right now: someone to hit.

And as he stood there, snarling and glaring down at her, Seven decided Ivan would serve beautifully in his capacity as her punching bag.

He was big and strong, and looked smug in a way that suggested he'd been training and was certain he'd win. But his lack of speed and overconfidence would work against him. She'd make sure of it.

Ivan made the first move, lunging at her and throwing a right hook that seemed to have all his weight behind it. If it connected, it would've shattered her jaw. But it didn't connect.

Seven dodged the blow, which threw Ivan off balance. When he stumbled, she stuck her leg out and tripped him. He hit the concrete floor face-first with a grunt of pain and a muttered Russian curse.

Ivan pulled himself to his feet, glared at her and snorted like an enraged bull. She shook her head. Fighting angry was the quickest way to lose.

He charged her, fists flailing. Seven was ready for him. She threw one straight punch to Ivan's gut, which doubled him over. Thinking of Benny's advice to make the fight more interesting for the crowd, Seven did a backflip, making sure to catch Ivan under the chin with her boot heel. The impact lifted Ivan right up off his toes. The crowd went wild when he landed flat on his back in the center of the cage.

Ivan scissored to his feet and bellowed in rage as he came at her once again. She dodged the hard left he threw at her, but shrugged her shoulder up to take the hit from his follow-up right. After all, Benny had told her it was unnatural for a fighter to never get hit. She wouldn't want the crowd to think she was even more of a freak than the vampires she'd been fighting lately.

A rumbling of unease rose from the crowd, followed by a shrill shriek of metal—and before Seven could process what was going on, she found herself staring down at the back of a snarling wolf who'd positioned himself between her and Ivan.

Ivan's eyes widened as he raised his hands. "I no fight shapeshifters," he muttered, then leapt back with a yelp when the wolf snapped and lunged at him.

Benny crawled into the cage through the giant gaping hole the wolf had left in its wake and grabbed Seven's arm. "Gotta go, doll," he hissed. "This ain't gonna end well."

"But he's still standing," she protested. "I'm not supposed to leave until one of us can't stand. You told me those were the rules."

He snorted as he dragged her away from the crowd and out into the alley behind the building. "Yeah, well, rules change when a pissed-off alpha shifter tears through the cage like he's the fucking Hulk and stakes his claim on one of the fighters."

She stumbled to a stop and blinked at him. "Wait. Was that *Lucas*?"

"Duh," he said with an eye roll. "Who'd you think it was? He all but peed on you in there to mark his territory."

"How am I his territory? He's in love with Harper."

Benny rubbed the back of his neck. "Doll, you never let me finish what I was sayin' that day at the bar. He used to have a thing for Harper, but now?" He shrugged. "He seems to only have eyes for you. And now we gotta go before he gets out of there and kills me."

A growl behind them had Benny spitting out every curse word Seven had ever heard.

Seven had never seen a fully shifted werewolf up close before. Anytime she'd had to eliminate them for Sentry she made sure she did so while they were in human form, since their strength after a shift was nearly double. But even in her limited experience, Seven would say that Lucas was an exceptionally good-looking wolf.

If he were to stand on his hind legs, he would be a foot taller than her, and his gray and black coat was so shiny he looked like he belonged in the high-end dog food commercial she'd seen while watching TV with Harper and Mischa the previous night.

But she imagined he probably wouldn't like that comparison.

Wolf Lucas coughed and spit out what appeared to be a scrap of tattered red nylon.

Ivan's athletic pants. Or what was left of them, at least. The wolf had obviously torn into Ivan a little while the big Russian was attempting to run away.

Benny tried to pull her back, but Seven knew better than to run from an enraged werewolf. A pissed-off wolf certainly didn't get *less* angry when he was forced to run down his prey. "Don't move," she said.

Benny chewed on his thumbnail. "This ain't good, man. This ain't good."

As they watched and waited, Lucas started shifting, snarling in what had to be agony as his muscles stretched and tore, his body reshaping itself back into human form. And when the change was complete and his eyes locked on hers, Seven had to agree with Benny.

This wasn't good at all.

CHAPTER SEVENTEEN

She stood her ground as he stalked toward her, chin tilted up, seemingly unconcerned that an out-of-control shifter had her in his sights. That show of strength and defiance pissed him off and turned him on in equal measure.

This woman was going to be the death of him.

"You're naked!" she blurted.

As unnecessary as that comment was, it eased Lucas's mind somewhat. She wasn't as calm as she appeared to be, which meant her self-preservation skills weren't so lacking that she didn't comprehend the danger he presented at the moment.

"Clothes don't normally survive a shift, doll," Benny muttered nervously. "Unless you're talking about the Hulk. I never was sure how his pants survived when all his other clothes kind of exploded off him. Did Bruce Banner have a tiny little pecker that didn't grow when he turned into the Hulk or somethin'? I dunno. Maybe—"

"Silence!"

Seven and Benny both flinched. He didn't blame them. Enough wolf remained in his voice that he barely sounded human.

He cut his glare to Benny. "Clothes. Find. Now."

"Y-yeah, OK. Come on, Seven. Let's—"

"She stays."

Benny blinked at him. "But are you sure you're—"

He snarled and took a menacing step forward. Benny let out a squeak, turned on his heel, and took off.

Seven didn't back down as he advanced on her, though. He stopped when they were toe-to-toe and she had to crane her head back to meet his eyes.

He had a million questions for her, but he was still too pissed off to formulate many words at the moment, so he settled for, "Why?"

Her eyes narrowed on him. "What difference does it make? As long as you have your *space*."

Lucas fought back another growl. Would that word haunt him for the rest of his fucking life? "I never *wanted* space. I said we *needed* space. And besides, the kind of *space* that has you fighting vampires every night in a fucking cage? Yeah, neither of us needs that *space*."

"None of these creatures are a danger to me," she said, sounding entirely too reasonable for his liking. "And I needed…"

"You needed?" he prompted.

"To hit something," she finished. "Finding out you're in love with Harper made me…angry."

Jesus, how had he fucked everything up this badly? "I'm not in love with Harper. I thought at one time I was…but I'm not."

Her eyes searched his with that laser-like intensity he'd come to expect from her before she murmured, "Truth."

He nodded and leaned toward her, putting his hands on either side of her head against the wall behind her. "I won't lie to you, Seven."

Her chin came up, her warm breath feathering across his cheek, her mouth only a heartbeat away from his. She lifted shaking hands and laid her palms flat against his chest. He nearly groaned out loud at the feel of those cool, delicate hands on his overheated skin.

She swallowed hard. "If you don't want *her*, then why don't you want *me*?"

Surely he hadn't heard her right. "You think I don't want you?"

Her gaze lowered to her hands on his chest. "I'm nothing like Harper. She's…open and funny and beautiful. I'll never be like her. I'm—"

"If you say *broken* I'm gonna be pissed," he said, fighting to keep from yelling at her. "You're not *broken*. You're *perfect*. So fucking perfect that it hurts not to touch you. Do you get that?"

Her eyes lifted to his and widened, and he was caught. He couldn't have looked away if his life depended on it.

They stayed like that for way, way too long, frozen as if they were seeing each other—*really* seeing each other—for the first time. He took a deep breath and the warm, slightly sweaty and entirely too sexy scent of her skin made him lightheaded. Her hands slipped down to his stomach as his chest moved. He couldn't hold back a hoarse groan.

Get out, he told himself. *Remember what Vi said. She needs space. Get out while you still can.*

She let her gaze drop to his mouth and she licked her lips.

"Fuck it," he muttered.

Then he kissed her.

Seven didn't really have any experience with kissing. The one time she'd decided to have sex was more out of curiosity than anything else, and kissing hadn't really been involved.

Now she knew what she'd been missing out on her whole life.

Lucas had always been tender with her, careful. But not now. He kissed her with an almost feral intensity that stole her breath, and his heart pounded against hers like a bass drum.

She wasn't sure what she loved more: the stretch and pull of his corded muscles and smooth, golden skin against her as he shoved her back against the wall, or the hot, wet slide of his tongue against hers. All she knew for sure was that she wanted more. And his low moan—not to mention the insistent press of his erection against her stomach—let her know he felt the same way.

Seven threaded her fingers through his hair and tugged him closer. Lucas growled low in his throat and moved his mouth more deliberately over hers. She was sure she'd ever tasted anything so amazing in her life. He tasted like peppermint and lust and need, and Seven wanted to devour him whole.

He slid his hands down her shoulders, along her ribcage, then slipped his fingertips beneath the snug bottom of tank top. Heat spread across her chest, her belly, and pooled between her thighs.

But still it wasn't enough. She wanted more. She wanted everything. All the passion and fire she'd been denied for so long. She wanted to absorb his heat and feel every inch of his bare skin beneath her greedy fingers.

Seven hitched a leg over his hip and ground against him in an effort to better fit her curves to the hard angles of his body. And still he wasn't close enough. Lucas must have sensed her struggle because he slipped his hands to her waist and lifted her. She wrapped both legs around his waist and moaned as her hips rubbed against his.

Together, they were a perfect fit.

Panting, he leaned into her, holding her in place with his weight as his hands shifted from her waist to her outer thighs, then up under her so that his hot palms were cupping her bottom.

Seven let her head fall back against the wall as his mouth slid down her neck. She gasped when his tongue dipped into the hollow at the base of her throat.

He left one hand on her bottom and used his other to tug down on her tank top. "God, you're so beautiful," he murmured.

So was he. Miles and miles of hot skin stretched taut over corded muscle. Masculine beauty at its finest.

He trailed teasing fingertips over the swells of her breasts, and her entire body tightened in anticipation. If he didn't touch her breasts fully she was going to scream, and then he did and she almost screamed anyway from the sheer pleasure of it.

The cool silk of his hair brushing against her throat, the warm strength of the hand that cupped her breast, the sharp pull of desire that rocked her as he flicked the tip of his tongue over her tightened nipple…God, it was almost more than her senses could handle.

And just when they'd gone as far as they could with her clothes still on, just when she was on the verge of begging him to drag her to the nearest bed and fuck her senseless…

A throat cleared, and someone said, "Wow, now I see why you needed these pants so bad."

Lucas rested his forehead against hers and muttered a curse. "Timing, Harper," he said through clenched teeth. "Yours could be better."

Harper grinned. Then she shrugged and said, "Yeah, I get that a lot."

CHAPTER EIGHTEEN

With supreme effort, Lucas forced himself to set Seven on her feet and release her.

Jesus, he'd been about two seconds away from fucking her against a wall, outside, in the middle of the shittiest part of town. What the hell was wrong with him? So much for his promise to Vi to keep his distance from Seven. And the worst part?

He'd do it again.

To distract himself from the fact that he was naked in an alley with a raging hard-on, he glared at Benny, who was trying—and failing—to hide behind Harper. "What the fuck, man? I told you to find clothes, not call Harper."

Jesus, anyone but Harper would've been preferable.

Benny threw up his hands in exasperation. "I didn't call Harper! I called Riddick 'cause he's about your size."

Ugh. He was wrong. Riddick was *definitely* less preferable in this situation.

Harper smirked at him. "You didn't think *I* could listen to a call where Benny says, 'Yo, Riddick, Lucas needs pants' and not show up, do you? I think you know me better than that. The comedy potential sounded like *gold*."

Benny rubbed his forehead. "Shit, I didn't think that through. Sorry, Lucas."

Then he pulled a pair of sweats and a T-shirt out of the messenger bag Harper was carrying. He squinted at them, then held them up for Harper's inspection. "What does Riddick have against colors, doll?"

"I don't know. He won't admit it, but I think he's color blind. He only ever wears black."

"Dude's like Johnny Cash, man."

"I know, right?"

Lucas face-palmed. "For the love of God, can you just toss me the clothes?"

"Sorry, man. Didn't mean to leave you hanging. Literally."

Harper snorted with barely suppressed laughter at Benny's joke, and Lucas kind of wanted them both dead at that particular moment.

Benny tossed him the clothes. "There you go. Feel free to tuck little Lucas away before the ladies are even further scandalized."

Seven's gaze immediately dropped to his dick. "Is *that* considered little?"

Harper and Benny dropped their gazes, too. "No," they said in unison. Seven looked really…interested, which wasn't helping him lose his hard-on.

"Jesus," Lucas muttered, not sure if he should be happy everyone agreed his dick wasn't small, or freaked out that everyone was studying his dick that closely. Was this really happening?

"It's just a figure of speech, hon," Harper explained to Seven.

"Oh," she said, frowning. "I don't really understand most of those. Especially in English. They never seem to make much sense."

"Yeah, English is tricky," Benny agreed. "I always liked Latin better."

Harper rolled her eyes. "You don't speak Latin, Benny. Pig Latin isn't the same thing."

"It ain't? Huh. Learn something new every day, I guess."

As Lucas pulled on the sweats, Harper said, "Hey, nice work on the cage in there, Lucas. It looks like the Kool-Aid man ran through it."

"Oh, yeah," Benny quipped in his best Kool-Aid man voice, then fist-bumped a giggling Harper.

Lucas suddenly felt about 700 years old. "Sweet Christ, you guys are immature. What the—"

"Get down!"

Lucas heard the shot pierce the night air a split second before Seven shoved him to the ground none too gently and dove on top of him. Benny tackled Harper, shielding her with his body as a second shot hit the wall behind them, showering brick shards down onto their heads.

The noise from the crowd that had been loitering in front of the foundry after the match grew to earsplitting levels. Lucas couldn't see them, but knew from the sound that they'd heard the shots and were panicking, screaming, running, and practically tearing each other apart in their attempts to escape.

"He's gone," Seven said in a shaky voice, unsteadily climbing to her feet.

"Jesus," Benny said, reaching down to help Harper up. "What the fuck was that?"

Lucas dusted off his borrowed sweat pants and looked back in the direction the shots had come from. "It sounded like a sniper rifle."

Harper ran a hand through her disheveled hair and frowned as her fingers got caught in the tangled curls. "Who the fuck were they shooting at?"

"Me."

Lucas looked back at Seven just in time to see her gingerly touch the back of her head, and frown as her fingertips came back coated in blood.

"Oh, shit," Benny whispered. "Seven…"

"No," Lucas grated out as he reached for her. "You can't be hit! You're bulletproof!"

She glanced down at the blood on her hand, looking confused and pale. So, so pale.

"I thought so, too," she murmured. "Huh. I guess I'm not."

His wolf's unholy howl ripped through the alley as she fell forward into his arms.

CHAPTER NINETEEN

The ER doc, a bedraggled fifty-something with smudged glasses, questionable stains on his scrubs, and a bedside manner only Stalin could love, worked furiously to stabilize Seven and assess her injuries. Even though the bullet had only grazed her, blood poured from the wound at the back of her head, quickly saturating every white gauze pad the doctor pressed against it.

Lucas didn't need the annoying beeping of the monitor to tell him her heart rate was lower than it should be. He could hear it himself. And he knew why.

The fucker had shot her with a silver bullet.

Dhampyres weren't violently allergic to silver like pure-blooded vampires, but they were sensitive enough to it that it dramatically slowed their healing process.

The doctor looked at Lucas over the tops of his glasses. "I need you to go to the waiting room." He gestured to the little blonde nurse who was scurrying around the room, gathering supplies. "We'll take care of her."

Lucas looked down at Seven—so pale, so tiny, so alone—in that bed, and immediately thought, *yeah, no fucking way*. He tightened his grip on her hand. "I'm not leaving her."

The nurse dropped the roll of gauze she was holding and her eyes widened in alarm. He couldn't say he blamed her. He was pretty sure his eyes were blazing yellow as he fought to keep his emotions—and his wolf—in check.

But the doctor, who'd obviously seen a thing or two in his day, looked unimpressed. "I'll call security if I have to," he said, his tone serious as a fucking heart attack.

Lucas met him glare for glare and bared his teeth in a mockery of a smile. There weren't enough rent-a-cops in the whole building to tear him from her side. "Good luck with that."

The stare down continued for a moment or two longer, until the doctor seemed to realize he'd need to call in the National Guard if he wanted to drag Lucas out of the room. He eventually sighed and grumbled, "Fine, but you need to stay out of our way while we take care of this head wound and figure out what to do about her heart rate. We don't get too many vampire hybrids here."

Behind him, Harper cleared her throat. "Just worry about the wound, doc. We can take care of the rest."

Lucas glanced back at her, brow raised.

"I called Leon," she said.

No further explanation was needed. Lucas immediately felt some of the starch melt from his spine.

Leon Steinfeld was Harper's office manager. But before that, he'd been a biochemist for Sentry. Leon and his group were directly responsible for the existence of *dhampyres*. He was a crooked, shady, unemployable-by-anyone-but-Harper little dude, but if there was anyone who'd know how to help Seven, it was Leon.

"I've got Benny back at the scene talking to witnesses, too," Harper added. "And Hunter and Mischa are talking to the fighters.

We'll find the shooter, Lucas. You don't have to worry about it being left up to the VCU."

He'd probably care about all that when he knew Seven was going to be alright. But right now? He found it hard to give a shit about anything but the woman who'd shoved him to the ground to keep him safe. The woman who'd taken a silver bullet to the back of the head while trying to protect *him.*

Seven shifted restlessly, moaning. Lucas braced his hands on either side of her head and leaned in close to listen. Her heart rate was increasing. Her eyes didn't open, but he could see her pupils moving underneath her lids.

Thank you, Jesus.

"Seven, sweetheart, time to wake up," he said. "Open your eyes for me. Can you do that?"

"Lucas," she said, barely above a whisper.

"That's right, sweetheart. How about you put me out of my misery and show me those gorgeous blue eyes of yours? What do you say?"

Her eyes fluttered open and locked on his. "Hi," she whispered.

For the first time since she'd passed out and fallen into his arms, he took an easy breath. He brushed her hair off her forehead, and let his knuckles brush over her cheek. "Hi, yourself."

The doctor elbowed Lucas in the ribs. "You need to move. We need to take some blood."

Lucas sat up and glanced over at the little man, who looked beyond exasperated as he stood there, syringe in hand. "Yeah, OK, sorry. I'll—"

"No!"

Seven jerked upright, grabbing Lucas's arm with one hand, flinging her free hand toward the doctor. The syringe shot out of his hand and flew across the room, slamming into the wall. The needle sank into the sheetrock up to the plunger.

"Holy shit," Harper murmured.

Holy shit's right.

If Seven's hand had made contact with the doctor's hand, the whole thing wouldn't have been so surprising. But…it hadn't.

The suddenly white-faced doctor glanced from his now-empty hand to the syringe sticking out of the wall, then back at his empty hand, visibly struggling to process what had just happened. The nurse traced a symbol of the cross over her chest.

Seven grabbed his T-shirt in two white-knuckled fists and buried her face against his chest. Tremors wracked her body. "Please don't let them touch me. I can't…just…no more."

The "please" damn near killed him. Lucas wrapped his arms around her, pressing her tight against his chest. "No more what, beautiful?"

"Needles," she whispered. "Experiments. No more. Please."

He closed his eyes as her words hit him physically, gnawing at his gut, knifing him in the heart. Jesus. So much pain.

You're goddamned right no more.

Logically, he knew she was hurt and disoriented, and she wasn't thinking clearly. This was a prime example of the PTSD Vi had warned him about. But she was clinging to him, trusting him to take care of her, and he wasn't going to let her down. Not now, not ever again.

Lucas unhooked the little clip on her finger that was connected to the annoying beeping machine, and scooped her up, cradling her against his chest. He looked at Harper, who had tears in her eyes. "We're leaving," he said, even though his jaw was clenched so tight it hurt.

Harper looked like she might argue, but eventually nodded. "Do you want to bring her to our place? Riddick can probably take care of that head wound for her."

He glanced down at the top of Seven's head. She still had her face buried in his shirt. "Can you let Riddick help you?" he asked her gently.

Her grip on him tightened and she shook her head. "I just want to go home. I don't want him to see me like this. Just please take me home."

The nurse hurried forward and handed Lucas a small plastic tube. "Liquid sutures," she explained. "Clean the wound—just use good old fashioned soap and water—and apply a little of this. The cut isn't that bad. Head wounds just always bleed a lot. She won't even need to come back for follow-up."

The doctor threw up his hands. "No idea why I bothered with medical school," he griped. "Guess I'm not needed here at all."

Everyone ignored him.

Lucas let out a relieved sigh. "Thank you," he said to the nurse, "for…understanding."

The nurse's smile was warm, if a little sad. "I've seen more than a few injured soldiers in my day." When he didn't respond, she asked, "She *is* a soldier, right?"

"Among other things," he said. "Among other things."

CHAPTER TWENTY

Harper, Riddick, Mischa, Hunter, Leon, and Benny were all together when Harper called Lucas later that night. It sounded like Haven was there, too, banging on some kind of toy, squealing gleefully every so often. With all the background chatter, it sounded like Harper was standing in the middle of Main Street at noon. During a parade. When the circus was in town.

So, pretty much, it was a normal night at Harper Hall's house.

"What do you have for me, Harper?" he asked.

"The fighters didn't see anything, but a few of the witnesses Benny talked to said the shooter was a white male, dark hair, about thirty years old, anywhere from six feet tall to six feet three, and anywhere from 180 to 210 ten pounds."

Fantastic. That narrowed it down to just about anyone in the world. "Vamp?"

"Human," she said.

Huh. That was surprising. If that was the case, the shooter probably wasn't a coven member of someone Seven had taken out when she'd worked for Sentry. So much for his best guess as to motive. "What else?"

"Well, not sure if this is helpful in any way, but one of the witnesses was apparently a gun aficionado and got a good look at the sniper rifle as the shooter was running away. Said it was a Dragunov."

A Russian weapon, Lucas thought. Semi-automatic, designated marksman rifle. A weapon like that wasn't just something the shooter had stumbled upon. It wouldn't have been easy to find, and it wouldn't have been cheap, which meant the shooter had a sniper rifle of choice that he'd gone to effort and expense to hunt down. He was a pro. And he hadn't been fucking around. He'd intended to blow her head off.

Jesus.

Lucas heard Harper flipping through the pages of what was probably Benny's notebook before she said, "And one witness said the guy had a weird tattoo on his forearm. Said it looked like a barcode."

Well, now *that* could actually be useful information. Maybe he wouldn't kill Benny after all.

"Ask him how she is," Lucas heard Riddick demand in the background.

Harper's muffled and somewhat annoyed reply: "She's fine or else he'd be all wolfed out, tearing the city apart instead of calmly talking to me."

He didn't hear what Riddick mumbled after that, but he imagined it involved something about dismembering Lucas if anything happened to Seven on his watch again. That seemed to be Riddick's current MO, at least. Lucas couldn't really say he blamed him, so he said, "Harper, tell Riddick his sister is fine; she's just resting. And put Leon on the phone."

"Well, certainly, but only because you asked so nicely," she replied tartly.

There was a shuffling noise on the line as Leon took the phone from Harper and said, "Yo, hey, man. How's it hanging?"

Leon and Benny's muffled laughter came over the line, letting him know the two of them had discussed Lucas's *Magic Mike* moment in the alley with Seven. Awesome.

Suddenly feeling the weight of the day pressing down on him to the point that he could barely breathe, he released a weary sigh and said, "You studied her brain scans, right?"

"I did. Her brain chemistry is…" he paused and let out a lusty sigh "…fucking amazing. Artwork. She's *extraordinary*."

"You should see her," Benny added. "*Scary* hot."

"Like that chick in *Spankenstein*?" Leon asked.

"Hotter," Benny said.

Thwack!

"Ouch!" Benny and Leon yelped in unison.

"Next time? I'm kneeing you both in the groin instead of just slapping the backs of your heads. No more porn talk!"

Lucas would've laughed at Mischa's statement if he wasn't currently the only one trying to stay on task. Shit like that lost its funny when he needed to focus.

"Leon," Lucas asked, "why did the bullet hurt her this time? I saw her stop a bullet with her bare hands at the prison. This one shouldn't have been able to hurt her."

"Well, based on her brain scan and what I know about her gene pool, I'd be willing to bet she's telekinetic."

Lucas suppressed an eye roll. "Yeah, Leon, we figured that out when she threw a syringe across the room without laying a finger on it."

"No, you don't get it," he replied. "Sentry didn't have any cleaners with that kind of power. None that they knew of, anyway. I'm betting she doesn't even know she has telekinesis. Throwing that syringe was probably an instinct. And that first bullet? I'm guessing she used her power without even realizing it to slow it down, then she just kind of plucked it out of the air. As a bystander, you wouldn't have even noticed. It all would've happened too fast."

Lucas rubbed his temple as he processed *that* new bit of crazy. "If the powers are triggered by some kind of survival instinct, why wasn't she able to stop the bullet tonight? And why didn't her *instincts* help her when she was in Midvale?"

"I have a theory on that," Hunter said in the background. There was another shuffling sound as Leon handed the phone over the Hunter. "I know from training Mischa to use *her* telekinesis that emotion greatly impacts control. If she's scared or emotionally overwhelmed, her powers can be unpredictable."

Harper snorted. "Yeah, if by *unpredictable* you mean blackout-the-whole-city-during-the-finale-of-*The-Walking-Dead* epic *failure*."

"Jesus," Mischa muttered, "will I ever live that down?"

"No," Harper answered.

Hunter ignored them and said, "I'm guessing that tonight, Seven was scared and was more concerned with protecting you than she was with protecting herself, so her power failed her."

Lucas closed his eyes. He'd been afraid of that. The thought of her putting herself in danger intentionally to protect him was scary as all hell. He couldn't let her do that ever again. "And what about when she was at Midvale?"

"You said she was drugged, right? I'd have to think drugs would impact her powers, as well."

Just thinking about the drugs and what had happened to her at Midvale had his wolf itching to break free again. Daniels better pray like hell that Lucas never saw him again.

"The good news," Hunter added, "is that I can help her. I can train her to use her telekinesis whenever she wants to, instead of just waiting for her survival instincts to kick in. We can start whenever she's feeling up to it."

That was all fine and good, but Lucas doubted she'd ever need her telekinesis again. Not with him glued to her fucking side. Because he'd be damned if he was going to let anyone hurt her again.

Hunter handed the phone back to Harper and she said, "Riddick and I will find the shooter, Lucas. Don't do anything stupid, OK?"

Stupid like hunting the fucker down himself and ripping out his damned throat? Watching and laughing while he bled to death in gut-wrenching agony? The thought hadn't even crossed his mind. Except maybe a few…thousand times or so.

Lucas said goodbye to Harper without promising anything and went to check on Seven. Her door was cracked open. Careful not to make any noise, he edged through the door.

Seven lay asleep in her bed, curled on her side with her knees drawn up to her chest like a child. She looked so peaceful, all her battle-hardened edges softened by sleep. As she shifted, the sheet covering her body slithered down, baring one moonlight-gilded shoulder to his hungry gaze.

The sight of her in that bed shook him harder than he cared to admit.

A frown line creased her brow and she moaned softly. His heart constricted. It seemed like she hadn't even been able to escape the day's events—or her past—in her sleep.

He wanted nothing more than to crawl into that bed with her, hold her against his heart, and chase her nightmares away. Slay her demons.

But her safety had to come first. He couldn't afford to get distracted. Her getting shot tonight had proven that to him. He'd been so distracted he hadn't even sensed the shooter. If she'd been killed…

Don't go there.

He'd let Harper do things her way. For now. And when Harper found the guy? That bastard would learn firsthand what an alpha werewolf was capable of.

Hunt.

Shred.

Trap.

Kill.

The shooter would never know what hit him.

CHAPTER TWENTY-ONE

"You're not beating me again."

Seven ignored Mischa's comment, which had been uttered through clenched teeth, instead choosing to keep her mind focused solely on the 500 pounds of free weights she was holding three feet off the ground behind her, using nothing but her telekinesis.

"Focus," Hunter reminded his wife.

He reminded her to focus a lot, Seven noticed. Mischa's emotions often got the better of her. Seven had no such problem. It was only her third day of training with Hunter and already, she had a fairly decent amount of control over her newly discovered talent.

Enough to beat Mischa, anyway.

Today, they were working in the completely tricked-out exercise studio in Hunter and Mischa's building. He had the two women facing each other, standing no more than a few feet apart, while they each held their own set of weights off the ground behind them. Whoever dropped their weights first lost the challenge.

Mischa's inability to focus didn't mean she was weak. Truth be told, her powers were much stronger than Seven's. And Seven was starting to feel like those free weights weighed a few thousand pounds instead of just a few hundred.

Seven's hands started shaking and she could feel sweat breaking out on her brow. Time to end this. She did the one thing she knew would tip the scales in her favor.

Seven smirked at Mischa. A cocky, easy smirk that said, *I can do this all day. Can you?*

Mischa's eyes narrowed on her and a growl of frustrated outrage ripped from her throat, followed by the deafening clang of her weights hitting the floor.

Seven let her own weights drop a second later and fell to her knees as her legs turned to mush. Mischa did the same.

Hunter gave them a slow clap. "Well done. Both of you. That was impressive."

Mischa groaned. "It was not. I got my ass kicked. Again!"

Hunter hoisted his wife off the ground as if she was weightless and let her sag against him. "Do you know why?" he asked.

"I lost my focus," she mumbled. "Again."

He chuckled and brushed a loose curl off her forehead. "You thought you were going to lose, you got frustrated, and your focus drifted."

Mischa pointed an accusing finger at Seven. "You baited me."

Seven would've nodded, but her muscles weren't responding yet. "Sure did," she wheezed out.

It took a minute, but Mischa eventually offered her a somewhat reluctant smile. "Good one. But just remember, tomorrow is sparring day. Paybacks are a bitch."

Seven looked forward to it. Sparring with Mischa was always an adventure. She sometimes sparred with Riddick and Hunter, but they tended to pull their punches, obviously not wanting to hurt her.

Mischa had no such compunction, which made her an ideal sparring partner.

Hunter offered Seven a hand and pulled her to her feet. "That's all for today. Do you need a ride home?"

"No, man, thanks anyway, but I've got her."

Seven turned to see her brother strolling into the studio.

Or should she say, her *babysitter*?

It had been a week since she'd been shot, and Lucas had made sure she was under constant guard. She'd tried over and over again to explain to him that it wouldn't happen again. She was ready for an attack now. She wouldn't be caught off guard again, and she could take care of herself. Thanks to Hunter's training, she was more capable than ever.

But Lucas was immovable.

When he wasn't available to babysit her, Lucas made sure Riddick or Hunter was with her. She couldn't even do a simple skip-trace with Benny without a hulking male shadow dogging her every step, which just made her targets run *that* much faster than usual.

But beyond the inconvenience and insulting implication that she was unable to protect herself, she was feeling…frustrated. Emotionally and sexually.

After that kiss in the alley—that full-body, mind-altering, soul-shattering kiss—she'd assumed that they'd pick up where they left off when they got home.

And where they'd left off was mostly naked.

Lucas hadn't made a single move to touch her or kiss her since that night. The emotional wall between them was firmly back in place, and it pissed her off and hurt her feelings in equal measure.

Seven was jerked out of her musings as Hunter and Mischa said their goodbyes and left her in the otherwise empty suite with her brother.

"What's wrong?" Riddick asked her.

"What makes you think something's wrong?"

He gestured to her eyes and forehead. "You're all scrunchy-faced again."

She sighed and sat down on a rolled up exercise mat. Riddick sat next to her, waiting. He was patient like that. While Harper or Benny or Mischa would push her for answers, Riddick waited quietly for her to speak at her own pace. She really liked that about him.

"I've never had family before," she began. "So, are there rules for what we can talk about and what we can't talk about?"

"Well, I've never had family before either, but from what I've learned from *Harper's* family, no, there are no rules. They'll pretty much talk about anything with each other."

Seven glanced over at him. "Can *I* talk to *you* about anything, Riddick?"

He thought about it for a second, looked a little nervous and nauseous at the possibility of deep conversation, then took a deep breath and said, "Yes. Sure. Whatever you need, Seven. I want to help. I'm here for you."

Truth. But that didn't really surprise her. Riddick had never lied to her, and something told her he never would.

With that in mind, she took a deep breath of her own and blurted, "How do I get Lucas to stop treating me like a little kid and start kissing me again?"

Riddick opened his mouth, then shut it again, shaking his head slightly. Eventually he said, "OK, we'll get to the kissing thing, but I need a minute to process that. So until then…um…how is he treating you like a little kid?"

"All we ever talk about anymore is how to secure wherever I'm going to be so that I don't get shot. He never asks about my day anymore, or watches TV with me. He's there with me, but…he's not *really* there. Does that make sense?"

He frowned. "It sounds like he's concerned about your safety, Seven. We all are. Aren't *you* concerned about your safety?"

She shrugged. "Not really. A day didn't go by with Sentry that someone didn't try to kill me. And I'm in better shape to defend myself now than I've ever been. I don't really understand why everyone's so worried all the time."

"This isn't like when you were with Sentry," he reminded her gently. "You're with people who care about you. And when you care about someone, you worry about their safety. It's just…what you do."

"You worry about Harper's safety?"

"Every damn day."

"But she's smart and capable and strong," Seven said. "She can take care of herself."

"I don't want her to ever *have* to take care of herself."

Seven glanced down at her clasped hands. "Because you…love her?"

"Yes."

"And…you love me, too?" she asked, still looking at her hands.

He caught her chin with his index finger and tipped her head gently so that she could meet his eyes. He smiled at her. "Yes. I do."

Her throat tightened around an annoying lump of emotion. "Do you think Lucas loves me?"

His smile drooped a bit. "I honestly don't know, sweetheart. But he'd be an idiot not to."

"I *want* him to love me," she admitted.

Riddick's nose crinkled up like he smelled something bad. "Yeah, I was afraid of that."

"You don't like him?"

"No, not really. But, I guess you could do worse," he admitted grudgingly. "He's not *all* bad."

"There's *nothing* bad about him. Except that he won't kiss me again."

Riddick rubbed the back of his neck. "OK, I was wrong. I don't really want to talk about the kissing." He shuddered. "But I can tell you this. Any idiot can see that he wants you. So if he's not kissing you, he's got a good reason. At least in his mind, it's a good reason."

She leaned forward. "What would be a good reason?"

"If I had to guess? I'd say he was protecting you from something. Maybe he doesn't think you're ready for a relationship? I don't know."

Seven frowned. "Shouldn't it be up to me to decide what I'm ready for?"

He chuckled. "You sounded exactly like Harper when you said that. And yes, it should be up to you to decide what you're ready for. But sometimes men can be stubborn assholes when it comes to stuff like that."

He sounded like he was speaking from experience, so Seven took him at his word. "So, what should I do now?" she asked.

Riddick stood up and offered her a hand. She let him pull her to her feet as he said, "If you want advice on how to get your man, it's time to retire the second string—*me*—and call in the big guns."

"You mean Harper, don't you?" she asked as Riddick slung an arm around her shoulders.

"Abso-fuckin'-lutely."

Lucas had told her that when it came to hugging, she'd eventually just know when the right moment was. He was right.

Twisting slightly, Seven wrapped her arms around Riddick's waist and rested her head on his chest. "Thank you," she whispered.

He was still a moment, but then his arms closed around her. "You're welcome, sweetheart," he said, his voice thick with emotion.

She thought for a moment. Riddick said love was taking care of someone because you didn't want them to have to take care of themselves. Vi had told her love was putting someone else's needs above your own, thinking of that person before you thought of yourself.

Well, that pretty much decided it.

"I love you, too, Riddick," she said quietly.

His grip on her tightened for a moment. "Everything's going to be fine, sweetheart. I promise."

As they walked out to Riddick's Harley arm in arm, he said, "You know that if he ever hurts you, I'll snap every bone in his body, right?"

She blinked up at him. "Is that another thing you *just do* for the people you love?"

"It is in this family, sweetheart."

CHAPTER TWENTY-TWO

About an hour later, the cavalry—Harper, her sister, Marina, and her mother, Tina—arrived at Lucas's house.

If Seven hadn't been told otherwise, she would've assumed these three women weren't related by blood. In contrast to Harper's slender, willowy form, Marina looked strong and athletic, curvy. And while she was built like Marina, Tina's teased cloud of platinum blond curls stood out in direct contrast to both her daughters' darker locks.

They all sat down in the living room, huddled together like football players during a timeout.

Harper clapped her hands together. "OK, we don't have much time because I have to pick Haven up from the sitter before six, so I'll sum up why we're here: Seven needs to get laid and we're here to help her get her man."

Marina raised a brow, incredulous. "We're here to help *her* get laid? On what planet can *she* not walk into a bar, crook her little finger, and *Pied Piper* her way out the door with twenty dudes?"

Tina frowned at her daughter. "Seven's a nice girl, Marina. She would never pick up men in a bar."

Seven wasn't sure what she'd ever said to give Tina the idea that she was *nice* girl, but she'd take the compliment. And given the way Tina's power wafted through the room like expensive perfume, Seven wasn't at all comfortable with the idea of disagreeing with Tina about, well, *anything* really. Empaths had always made her nervous. And even among other empaths, Tina was extraordinarily powerful.

"Seven doesn't want to pick up men in a bar," Harper explained patiently. "She wants Lucas."

Marina's eyes widened. "Lucas? You mean Lucas *Cooper*? The cop? The crazy-hot one who looks like the love child of Wolverine and Jamie Lannister?"

"Yep," Harper said, making a popping sound on the "p". "That's him. He's into her, too, but he's slow as Christmas making his move for some reason."

Marina's eyes drifted over to Seven. "Lucky bitch," she said, sounding awed.

Seven didn't take it personally. If she was able to pull this off, she *would* be a lucky bitch.

"So, Marina," Harper said, "you're on hair and makeup."

Marina nodded and pointed to what looked a fishing tackle box that she'd left by the door. "I brought my stuff, but I don't know how much I'm gonna need." She studied Seven's face, then scowled. "I'm used to making the old crones on the morning show look like they aren't tragic plastic surgery victims. I'm not sure I know what to do with *this* kind of canvas. I mean, shit, she doesn't have one single visible pore!"

"Just keep it light," Harper advised. "Enhance, don't spackle. And natural but pretty with the hair. Nothing fancy."

"Gotcha."

Harper pointed at her mother. "You're on dinner. Did you bring the stuff for your lasagna?"

"Sure did," Tina said, then patted Seven's knee. "Don't you worry, dear. Nothing puts a man in the mood faster than a good meal. People get *pregnant* after eating my lasagna."

Harper wrinkled her nose. "Gross, Ma. That makes it sound like there's magic sperm in the sauce or something."

Tina pursed her lips. "Well, of course there's not *sperm* in the sauce. I just mean that my lasagna puts men in an *amorous* mood. Why, the first time I made it for your father, he—"

Marina clapped her hands over her ears. "La-la-la," she sang loudly. "I can't hear you. La-la-la."

Tina opened her mouth to speak, but Harper silenced her by holding a hand up in front of her face. "I *beg* you not to finish that sentence. Beg. Seriously."

With a few additional exasperated, under-the-breath comments about ungrateful wretches, Tina made her way to the kitchen to begin cooking.

Marina led Seven to the bathroom and had her sit on the toilet seat lid while she unpacked her travel kit. Harper grabbed an armful of clothes and stood in the doorway explaining the different perks and drawbacks of each prospective outfit while Marina worked on her hair and makeup.

An hour later, the nearly orgasmic smell of Tina's lasagna filled the air and Seven barely recognized the woman in the mirror.

"Wow," she breathed, leaning towards the mirror, staring at her reflection with wide eyes.

Behind her, Marina smiled. "I know, right? Do I do great work, or what?"

Seven nodded slowly. "It's…wow."

Marina reached over and continued to fluff Seven's hair while she spoke. "I only snipped about two inches off the ends, but taking even that much extra weight off lets your natural curl spring up a little. After that, I just did a little side part—which is totally sexy on you, by the way—added some gel, dried it with a diffuser and voila!"

Seven had no idea what a diffuser was and had never used gel, but even she couldn't argue with the results.

Her dark brown hair was usually a heavy, somewhat frizzy, tangled mass of waves that she'd taken to wrestling into a ponytail each morning so that it didn't get in her face while she was working or training. But with Marina's help, it was smoother, lighter, and significantly…fluffier. The curls were looser than Harper's, but pretty and feminine nonetheless.

"It's gorgeous, Mar," Harper said from her spot in the doorway. "What did you do to her face? It doesn't even look like she's wearing makeup."

"Just tweezed the brows a bit—you'll need to do that from now on, girl. Don't let them start growing together like that again—and added a little contour color to highlight those *ridiculously* high cheekbones, finished it all off with a few swipes of mascara and some lip gloss."

"Voila," Seven whispered, still entranced by the stranger in the mirror.

"Yep," Marina agreed, somewhat smugly. "Voila."

Giving her head a shake, Seven glanced down at her dress. She'd never worn a dress before. It felt strange to have practically the entire length of her legs exposed. "Harper, are you sure about this dress? I could always just wear my—"

"No!" Harper and Marina answered in unison. "You're wearing that dress," Harper added, her tone leaving no room for argument. "It was *made* for you."

Marina said, "If he doesn't jump you tonight, he's gay. Or his dick's broken. Trust me, looking like that, you're getting laid tonight."

Tina glanced at her over Harper's shoulder. "Oh, sweetheart, you look lovely. That boy doesn't stand a chance. He'll be drawn to you like Winnie the Pooh to a honey pot."

Harper pulled a disgusted face. "Don't say *honey pot* when we're talking about sex, Ma."

Marina snickered while Tina scowled and said, "How is it that you girls can turn even the most innocent of comments into a sexual innuendo?"

"God-given talent," they said in stereo, then laughed and shouted, "Jinx!" at each other.

Seven wished she could laugh with them, but at the moment, a lump of emotion and self-doubt was threatening to cut off all her air. Her self-doubts were annoying like that. She could be perfectly happy, starting to feel *normal*, and the doubts would come up out of nowhere and smack her in the face, reminding her that if these people—this *family*—had any idea what she'd done, what she'd *been*, they would never be willing to stand by her side again.

"Oh, no you don't," Tina said, elbowing Harper out of the way.

Grabbing her chin and forcing eye contact, Tina stared Seven down and said in a stern voice that completely belied her soft appearance, "I won't allow you to start feeling sorry for yourself. You will *not* doubt yourself ever again. The kind of person you were when you were with Sentry? You were the kind that *survived.* Did what you had to do in order to *survive.* You had no choice. Do you understand me?"

Seven could only nod dumbly.

"Shit," Marina mumbled, stuffing her make-up and hair accessories back into her travel kit. "She broke out the mom voice."

Tina ignored her and continued speaking to Seven as if they were alone in the room together. "Do you forget who you're with, child? You're here with the best empath and psychic," she gestured to Harper, "Sentry ever had. The reason it's so easy for us to accept you? First of all, we're not that different. Harper and I both did things for Sentry we aren't proud of. Like you, we had no choice. You are no less deserving of love and happiness than we are. And second of all? We've already *felt* and *seen* the type of person you are. You can't hide anything from the two of us."

"It's true," Harper added. "I didn't want to say anything, but when I first hugged you? At the office? I picked up visions, just flashes really, of what happened to you at Midvale. And also some flashes of your past assignments with Sentry. From what I saw? You only did what you had to do. You never had a choice."

"There's always a choice," Seven said quietly.

"Given the information put in front of us by Sentry at the time, how could any of us have made different choices?" Tina asked.

Harper sighed when Seven didn't reply. "Well, if you don't believe us, maybe you'll believe Hunter. As head of the Vampire Council, he has access to all of Sentry's records. I had him look into your…clean-ups."

Clean-ups, Seven thought. What a lovely euphemism for *kills*.

"I looked at every one of them, Seven," Harper went on. "Every single one of them. And if I'd been in your shoes, I wouldn't have done anything differently. Hunter agreed with me."

Tina let go of Seven's chin and rocked back on her heels. "See how we're not that different after all?"

Seven closed her eyes and focused on the sounds of their breathing, their heartbeats. They were telling her the truth. They knew all her secrets and accepted her anyway. And if they accepted her, didn't it make logical sense that she should start accepting herself?

It's what Lucas and Vi and Riddick had been telling her all along. It all made sense. And it was so simple! These people loved her, faults and all. They'd support her no matter what, and she'd do the same for them.

"Holy shit," she blurted. "I really *am* part of your family now, aren't I?"

There was a loaded pause before Tina, Harper, and Marina all burst out laughing.

"As if there was ever any doubt," Tina finally said, giving her a motherly hug.

Marina smirked. "So, we should bring her to the next family dinner? Introduce her to the rest of her family?"

Harper groaned. "Let's not scare the girl off just yet, okay?"

CHAPTER TWENTY-THREE

He'd spent days—hours and hours of his life he'd never get back—following up on one unreliable eyewitness account after another, and Lucas was no closer to finding out who'd taken that shot at Seven than he'd been when he started investigating. Mischa and Hunter apparently weren't having any better luck checking things out on their end, either.

The shooter was a ghost. Fucking Casper.

Lucas was, however, willing to admit that maybe his investigative skills weren't currently at their finest. He hadn't slept more than an hour here and there since Seven was hurt. Between obsessively checking the locks on all the windows and doors while she was *in* the house and making arrangements to ensure she was never alone when she *left* the house—not to mention the time he spent at work following leads—his free time was pretty much nonexistent. And sleep was the last thing on his to-do list.

But while he was running around like a crazy man, the one thing he did have plenty of time for was thinking. And all that thinking led him to a conclusion he would've figured out long ago if he wasn't such a dumbass.

He loved Seven.

She was on his mind constantly and he didn't want to be away from her for even a minute. He didn't care what obstacles they had to overcome—be it external or internal obstacles—he wanted her.

Finally admitting it to himself, realizing that everything he'd ever wanted and assumed he'd never have was within in his grasp was exhilarating. Freeing.

And fucking *terrifying.*

He should've just been honest with her from the start about Vi's advice and how he was feeling. They could've worked through whatever came up together. He hadn't given Seven nearly enough credit.

How the hell was he going to convince her to give him a chance now? He'd been such a damned idiot for so long, all tied up and twisted in knots over nothing. He shook his head, disgusted with himself.

Ugh. That's enough deep thoughts on no sleep and no food.

More ready than he'd ever been to fall into bed and not crawl back out for a solid twelve hours, Lucas started to punch in the security code on his front door, only to leap back when someone on the inside threw the thing open, nearly braining him.

"Jesus, Harper," he muttered.

"Sorry," she said, not sounding *at all* sincere. "If her face is scrunchy tomorrow, I'm going to let Riddick break both your legs. He's been dying to do that, anyway. It'll totally make his day."

"Okay," he answered on autopilot. He had no idea what she was talking about, but more times than not, Harper's explanations just confused him even more. Better to just roll with it.

Harper nodded as if they'd come to an agreement, and marched past him without another word.

Her sister Marina trudged out after her, carrying an armful of dresses and a…tackle box? What the hell were these women up to?

Marina stopped in front of him, looked him up and down in a way that vaguely made him feel like a tasty, plated dessert, let out a deep sigh, and grumbled, "Lucky bitch," before walking away, shaking her head.

Tina was the next one out the door. He straightened up a little when she looked up at him. "Ma'am," he said with a slight tip of the head.

"I'm glad you finally got your head out of your ass where my daughter is concerned, dear," she said matter-of-factly.

"Um…thank you?"

"The two of you never would've worked out, you know."

"I know."

Well, he knew that *now*, at least. Better late than never, right?

She reached up and pinched his cheek—actually *pinched his cheek* like his grandmother used to do to him when he was a little kid—and gave a fond, motherly smile. "Now, just make sure you don't fuck everything up tonight, all right, sweetheart?"

And with that, she gave his cheek one final pat—none too gently, he might add—and left him standing by his front door, completely baffled.

If he lived to be a thousand, he was pretty damn sure he'd still never understand women. Especially not any of the women in Harper's family.

In the foyer, he took a moment to greet a particularly happy-looking Lucky, who was drooling like Pavlov's dog. It only took Lucas a second to figure out why.

The heavenly scents of garlic, melted cheese, tomato, and basil wafted from the kitchen. His stomach growled and he might've drooled a little himself in response. Tina's lasagna, he recognized immediately. His absolute favorite food on the planet.

A fact that he planned to take to his grave. If asked in a court of law, he'd swear on a stack of Bibles that his favorite food was his mother's meat loaf. He'd never admit otherwise aloud.

"Fuck yes," he muttered. About damn time something went his way today.

Food and sleep on his mind, he followed his nose to the kitchen…and froze mid-step when he caught sight of Seven a few feet away, standing next to the dining room table.

His eyes were so confused. He had no idea where to look first. Soft, subtle makeup, sexy side-parted curls trailing down over smooth shoulders, glossy red lips, and the dress…

Jesus. Christ.

The dress was halter-style, a bold shade of fuck-me red, and was cut low enough in the front to display a hint of cleavage, but not enough to reveal *too* much. The skirt of the dress flirted with the tops of her knees, but was slit high on either side, giving him a damn-near mesmerizing glimpse of her firm, toned thighs.

His gaze lowered and he couldn't help but smile. She was wearing her shit-kicking Doc Martens with her elegant, high-end dress.

She followed his gaze down to her shoes and she bit her lower lip. "The shoes Harper suggested I wear were highly impractical."

"Those are perfect," he rasped, surprised he could even form words he was so fucking turned on. "You're beautiful."

Seven smoothed her skirt and shrugged. "Marina did the hair and makeup. The dress is Harper's. I probably would've just worn my regular clothes."

Which would've been perfectly fine and a great travesty all at the same time. She was gorgeous in her regular clothes, but in this dress…damn.

"In fact," she went on, "I'm thinking I should just go change…"

Her nervous spill of words halted when he moved toward her, grabbed her hand and lifted it to his mouth, brushing his lips gently across her knuckles. "I wasn't talking about the hair, makeup, or dress. *You're* beautiful. Don't you dare change *anything*."

And just when he was pretty sure that was a crazy understatement and that he'd never seen anything so beautiful in his life, her eyes lifted to his and she smiled. That smile pretty much decimated what was left of his thoughts. If he had to remember his own damn name at this point, he was reasonably certain he couldn't do it.

"Are you hungry?" she asked, gesturing to the table. "There's a ton of food."

Food? What the hell was that? He was pretty sure there was nothing in the world other than this perfect woman in front of him.

Then his stomach rumbled. Loudly.

Oh, yeah. *Food.*

Her smile slipped into a smirk. "I'll take that as a yes," she said.

Good thing. Especially since he hadn't exactly found his tongue yet.

CHAPTER TWENTY-FOUR

Seven leaned back in her chair, more stuffed than she'd ever been. "I can't believe I ate all that," she said, amazed.

Lucas mimicked her posture. "I know, right? I swear to God she puts heroin in that stuff. There's no other way to explain how addictive it is. I quit being hungry twenty minutes ago, but kept eating anyway. God bless that woman."

"She scares the crap out of me," Seven admitted.

"Me too. I'm pretty sure she scares the crap out of everyone."

They'd talked about more in the past hour than they had in weeks, Seven realized. Lucas's emotional wall was as low as it was ever going to be.

She took a deep breath. It was now or never.

"Can we talk about something important?" she asked.

"Yeah. I was wondering if you were ever going to explain all this," he said, gesturing to the table, then to her.

He didn't look nervous about talking with her, or nauseated like Riddick looked when he was forced to talk to anyone. That was a good sign, she decided. And on Harper's advice, she'd spent a fair amount of time planning out what she was going to say.

So, feeling pretty confident in her plan, she said, "I did all this to get you to have sex with me."

Lucas choked on the mouthful of beer he'd just swallowed.

She blinked at him. Well, that was unexpected. She hadn't meant to say *that* at all.

He wiped his mouth on the back of his hand, staring at her with a shocked expression. Shock and…something else. She wasn't sure what. Horror, probably.

"I don't know why I said that," she mumbled. "I didn't mean to say anything about sex until much later in the conversation." She stood up, her movements jerky. "I'm just going to go start the dishes—"

Seven gasped as Lucas grabbed her hand and tugged her down into his lap.

"You can't drop that kind of bombshell on me and run away," he said, his voice lower than usual. "I need a minute to think because what you said made all the blood leave my brain."

Truth. And not because her powers told her so. She could feel *very clearly* where his blood had gone when it left his brain. Huh. Maybe she hadn't wrecked everything after all.

After a long, long pause, he shifted her so that she was sitting sideways on his lap and said, "I don't want to have sex with you."

The hard on beneath her would disagree, she thought, but the words were like an icepick to her heart nonetheless. "OK. I'll just—"

His arms banded around her when she moved to stand up again, locking her in place. "I'm not done."

His eyes were locked on hers, and the longer he held her gaze, the warmer she felt. He looked so serious that her breath got caught in her throat.

"I don't *just* want to have sex with you," he clarified.

"What do you want?" she asked, barely recognizing her own voice. She was pretty sure she'd never sounded so breathy in her life.

"I want everything."

Her eyes widened. "Everything?"

He leaned forward and rested his forehead against hers. "Everything. Look, I don't want our first time together to be about raging hormones," he said, letting his fingertips slide under the hem of her skirt to rest on her thigh. "I want to make sure we're on the same page."

Our first time. That sounded good. It implied there would be many, many other times. She gave in to temptation and slid her hand into the collar of his shirt, sighing as her fingertips met the warm skin and corded muscle of his shoulder. She could only imagine how amazing his skin would feel against her own.

"You sound like Violet," she said. "Do we have to talk about our feelings now?"

He moaned and his fingers tightened on her thigh. "If you keep touching me, I probably won't be capable of talking for much longer, so I better go first."

She liked that, too. The thought that *she* had that kind of power over *him*? It made her feel sexy, bold, and more beautiful than any makeover ever could.

She also liked that her lips were so, so close to his. All she had to do was…

"I've had *just sex* plenty of times before."

Seven frowned. Wow, the word "plenty" had a strangely ice-water-like effect on her libido. And she wasn't quite sure what that had to do with anything. "I had *just sex* once before, too," she said.

"With who?" he asked, sounding surprised—which was a little insulting—and possibly a little jealous.

"Another cleaner." She shrugged. "I was curious."

He pulled back enough to look her in the eye and raised a brow. "Curious? And what did you think?"

"It was pleasant."

"Pleasant?"

Nodding, she said, "Very…pleasant."

"Well, good to know where the bar's been set," he muttered, then gave his head a hard shake. "Sorry. That wasn't where I wanted this conversation to go. I meant to say that shifters— wolf shifters, anyway—can have sex all they want, but they only truly mate once, and that's for life."

She already knew that. She'd known what he was insinuating from the moment he said he wanted more than just sex. He wanted her to be his mate. She *wanted* to be his mate. So why were they still talking when they could be…mating?

With that in mind, she leaned in and pressed a small kiss against the corner of his mouth.

A muscle in his jaw jumped and his whole body went still beneath her. "Do that again," he growled.

His voice was rough, hard, and she wasn't sure if he was making a demand or issuing a dare. And she wasn't sure she cared.

Seven slid her other hand into his hair and kissed him again. Only this time, it wasn't just a chaste press of her lips against his. She ran her tongue across his lower lip, taking her time.

Lucas shuddered. His hands shifted, one moving into her hair to cup the back of her head, and the other sliding down to the base of her spine.

"Are you trying to distract me?" he asked in a rough whisper.

She cocked her head to one side and thought about it for a moment. "That wasn't my intention. But…am I?"

"God yes."

"Do you want me to stop?"

"God no."

Seven couldn't help but smile at what felt like a huge victory. She sucked his bottom lip into her mouth, pressing her teeth into the soft skin just hard enough to let him know she was serious.

And that was all it took to break his control.

Lucas's mouth moved over hers as if he'd been starving for her his whole life. His hands tightened on her as if he couldn't get close enough.

Yes.

This is what she'd been wanting ever since that night in the alley…this overwhelming pleasure, heady desire. It consumed her, let her forget about everything and everyone else in the world.

Seven squealed when he stood up abruptly, taking her with him. One sweep of his hand cleared the table, sending plates and food and glasses crashing to the floor.

Lucas set her on her feet, only to flip her around so quickly she had to brace herself on the kitchen counter. His hands roamed her back, found her zipper, and slid it down. He made a hungry noise somewhere between a growl and a groan as the dress puddled at her feet, leaving her completely naked, except for her boots.

"Harper said the underwear I usually wear would show through the dress, so I decided not to wear any," she explained breathlessly.

"God, I love the way you think."

He grabbed a fistful of her hair and pulled it aside, exposing her skin, then he trailed open-mouthed kisses across her shoulder, up to her ear, and back down again, voraciously, like a starving man.

His hands—God, his *hands*…work-roughened and so warm and strong and perfect, driving her absolutely crazy—were everywhere, fingers bumping over every rib, smoothing over her stomach, sliding over her breasts…she lost count of all the places he touched her, and still it wasn't enough. She wanted more.

She wanted *everything.*

Seven reached back and grabbed his hips with both hands, pulling him tighter against her. And when he bent his knees and rolled his hips into her, she cried out—a desperate, hungry sound that he prolonged by kneading her breasts and rubbing his thumbs over her tightened nipples.

"Please," she finally begged.

"Tell me what you want."

"I want everything," she choked out. "I want everything with you."

His hum of approval vibrated through her entire body, raising goosebumps in its wake. Her fingertips tightened on his hips and she sucked in a deep breath when he nudged her legs apart with his knee.

Lucas cupped her jaw with one hand and tipped her head to the side so he could capture her mouth with his. And his other hand…oh, his other hand. It slid down between her breasts and over her belly, clearly determined to make her melt into a puddle of want and need right there on the floor at his feet.

Of their own volition, her hips bucked forward. And clearly her hips knew what they were doing, because the movement caused his middle finger to glide over her clitoris, setting her entire body on fire.

He swallowed her broken, needy howl and his erection jerked against her back, hard as iron and insistent. She wanted him more than she'd ever wanted anyone or anything in her life. She wanted him as wild as she felt, as he *made* her feel. But still he insisted on moving his finger in slow, gentle circles over her clit.

That just wasn't enough anymore.

Seven grabbed his hand and shoved it lower, showing him exactly what she wanted.

His growl of approval mingled with her sharp cry of pleasure as he parted her, sliding easily along her slick folds, and plunged two fingers deep inside.

God, yes.

She'd imagined what having him touch her like this would feel like. The reality of him was *so* much better than her imagination. His fingers were hot and rough and exactly what she needed, exactly where she needed them.

She wanted to tell him to cup her breast with his free hand, but coherent speech was outside her control at the moment. Thankfully, he seemed to know her body better than she did because he did it without being told. Thank God. It seemed all she was capable of doing at the moment was clinging hard to his hips in an effort to remain on her feet.

He played her body so expertly—fingers dipping and sliding in and out of her, palm applying *just* the right amount of pressure to her clitoris—that she was already embarrassingly close to orgasm.

Being out of control—especially *this* out of control—was so foreign to her that she knew a moment of panic. Instinct told her to pull herself together, turn around and take what she wanted from him. Don't let him know the kind of power he had over her body.

She tried to turn in his arms. Maybe if she took a moment to come to her senses, to level the playing field a little, she'd feel better.

But Lucas didn't let her have it. He wrapped his arm around her, just under her breasts, pulling her back against him in a vice-like grip she doubted she could've broken even if she was at full strength. And at the moment? She was far, *far* from at full strength.

"Come now," he ordered, his hot breath sliding along her throat where his lips and teeth were busy working even more dark magic on her poor, untried senses.

She shook her head and bit her lip, but when his fingers picked up their wicked pace and he gently bit the skin where her shoulder met her neck, she was lost. Seven gasped and arched back against him, control all but a memory as she tumbled headlong into the first wave of her orgasm.

She convulsed in his grip, heard sounds she was pretty sure she'd never made before in her life falling from her lips. And still Lucas didn't pull back. Instead, he pushed her higher, faster, forcing her to feel every throbbing, bone-melting second of her release, making it last as long as possible.

When it was all over, when the last wave of her release rolled through her, when she was completely unraveled from top to bottom, she went limp. He swept her up into his arms and starting walking toward his bedroom.

"More?" he whispered, looking down at her with hot, hungry eyes.

Could she take more? He'd almost killed her with nothing more than a few kisses and his hands on her body. He *owned* her with nothing more than a few kisses and his hands on her body. Could she handle all of him?

This was Lucas, she reasoned. Lucas who took her in when no one else could. Lucas who rescued her from the bowels of hell. Lucas who checked on her every night when he thought she was asleep to make sure she was safe.

There was really only one answer she could give.

"Everything," she whispered back. "Give me everything."

CHAPTER TWENTY-FIVE

They should be talking, Lucas realized. He'd said he didn't want their first time to be all about raging hormones, and he'd pretty much done nothing *but* let his hormones get the best of him all night.

But he was too far gone now to talk. Truth be told, he'd been too far gone the moment he saw her in that dress, looking happy and hopeful and so damned beautiful it hurt—actually hurt—not to touch her.

They'd talk later.

Much, much later.

Right now his thoughts were pretty much solely of the *take, mark, mate* variety. The man was still in control, but the wolf wanted his say in the matter, too. And both the man and the wolf wanted Seven.

His blood pounded through his veins as he deposited her on the bed and gazed down at her.

Watching her while she'd come apart in his arms, learning what she liked, what drove her crazy, finding his own pleasure in giving her what she needed…he'd never felt anything like it. He'd never felt more powerful than he had in that moment.

And, Jesus, was there anything more beautiful in the world than Seven, flushed and happy and satisfied, gazing up at him through lids that were at half-mast, waiting for him to join her in that bed? If there was, he'd certainly never fucking seen it.

Her breasts were flawless. Firm and round, large enough to fill his hands, with tight pink nipples that made his mouth water for a taste. And her waist was so tiny he was pretty sure he could span it with his hands. Or maybe it only appeared that way due to the rounded flare of her hips. Whatever the case, she was breathtaking, and there were about a million ways he wanted to fit that tight, perfect body against his.

He had no idea what the hell he'd done in this life to deserve such beauty, but he certainly wasn't going to question it.

She squirmed on the bed and reached a hand out toward him. "Now," she whispered urgently.

Lucas shook his head and grinned down at her. "I've waited forever for you. There's no way I'm rushing this."

Her growl of frustration was the sexiest thing he'd ever heard in his life.

And that was his last thought before he found himself tossed through the air. He landed flat on his back on the bed.

Before he could so much as blink, Seven was on him, straddling his waist, gazing down at him with a mix of triumph and lust and need shining in her eyes that was so damn beautiful it took him a minute to comprehend what had just happened.

"Was that…did you just…Seven, did you just use your telekinesis to throw me onto the bed?"

She caught her lower lip between her teeth. "Yes."

He thought about that for a moment, before saying, "God, that's hot."

Seven let out a relieved breath, followed quickly by a loud, needy moan when he leaned up, cupped one of her breasts and sucked on the nipple of the other. Arching her back to give him better access, she fisted her hands in his shirt and ripped it wide, scattering buttons all around them.

A few minutes later, he found out that Seven could also use her powers to take off his pants and tattered shirt, all while taking off her own shoes, kissing him senseless, and running her hands over every muscle on his chest and abdomen. Telekinesis was a beautiful, beautiful thing, he thought when they were finally skin-to-skin from top to bottom.

Seven slithered down his body, leaving a trail of warmth and hot, wet kisses in her wake. She took his cock in her tiny hand and peered up at him from beneath thick, dark lashes, her eyes silently questioning.

Yeah, like he was going to stop her.

Her lips brushed over him, light, teasing. He slid his fingers into her hair, close to the scalp, and gaped down at her. Lucas was fairly certain he'd never seen anything as intensely erotic and stunning as Seven when she tipped her eyes up to him and sucked his length between her red lips. He choked out a harsh breath as the wet heat of her mouth wrapped around him.

"Jesus Christ, Seven…"

His fingers tightened against her scalp, tangling in her curls. His body was screaming for him to thrust into her mouth, but he resisted. He wanted her to control this, and he didn't want to finish like this. And he was already too close to the edge, walking a very thin line.

Very. Thin.

"So fucking good," he rasped.

She moaned around him and he shivered at the sensation. The suction of her mouth, the flicks of her hot tongue…Jesus, if he didn't make her stop now, he was going to lose it.

Lucas tightened his hold on her hair and eased her head back. She looked up at him, lips swollen and wet.

"Did I do something wrong?" she asked.

"Fuck no," he said, his voice practically strangled by lust. "I just can't take much more of that or I'll lose control."

Her answering smile went straight to his dick, which jerked toward her with an eagerness that was downright embarrassing.

"What if I want you to lose control?" she asked.

She gasped as he reversed their positions, dumping her on her back on the mattress beneath him.

"You first."

CHAPTER TWENTY-SIX

Seven's heart was pounding a staccato tattoo on her breastbone. She'd loved being in control for that brief moment, drawing that deep groan out of Lucas when she'd taken the hot, heavy weight of him in her mouth. His ragged breathing and the way his hand tightened reflexively in her hair was thrilling.

She'd almost resisted when he stopped her and forced her to release him. But she was so eager to have him inside her that it had been little more than a fleeting thought.

Lucas crawled up her body slowly, letting his eyes rake over her along the way. He was holding his weight off her so that they were barely touching, but his gaze was so intense and full of something she couldn't quite name—awe? Adoration? Some mix of both—that she felt it as surely as if his hands had followed the same path. All she knew for sure about that look was that it made her feel cherished and needed in a way she'd never felt before.

And then he smiled down at her—a smile so full of sex and sin that she shivered—and settled himself between her thighs, the width of his shoulders spreading her wide.

Then, without warning, his head dipped down and he slid his tongue through her wet folds, his gaze locked on hers all the while.

Her mind went completely blank and every muscle and sinew in her body tightened. She felt that lick through her entire body, from head to toe.

"Oh my God," she choked out.

She felt him smile against her inner thigh. "You taste incredible," he said. "Just like I imagined."

He'd imagined this? She never could've imagined anything *this* incredible in a million years.

He lowered his head again, licking, kissing, and nipping at her sensitive, over-heated flesh again and again.

Seven's hands fisted in the sheets beneath her. Her hips bucked of their own volition. Incoherent pleas fell from her lips. He responded to her body's cue, increasing his pace. Her body, her pleasure, was his to command.

"Will you come for me again?" he asked.

She opened her mouth to tell him yes, *God yes*, whatever he wanted her to do she would, but she lost her words to a deep moan when he slid his thumb hard over her clit while his tongue dipped into her.

And that's all it took to break her.

Her entire body clenched and she gasped for breath as she came so hard it bordered on painful. And still he didn't let up, continuing his assault on her oversensitive skin, making her orgasm last until she wondered if she could actually die from too much pleasure.

Seven couldn't find the energy to raise up on her elbows, but she managed to turn her head to the side to watch him stand up and pull a condom from the bedside table. He was so beautiful. All taut, lean muscle and golden skin, long lines and predatory grace. If she could move, she'd explore every one of those muscles and every inch of that skin.

He tossed the wrapper aside and rolled the condom down his length. Seven watched, transfixed. There was something so…erotic about the sight of his hands on his own body.

But she didn't have long to ponder the thought before he crawled over her once again, this time lowering onto her.

He cupped her head in his hands as he stared down at her. "Are you sure?"

She nodded, shifting restlessly beneath him, grabbing his hips with both hands. "Very. I want you."

It was a gross understatement. In truth, she'd never wanted anything more.

She felt a tremor run through him at her words. His eyes fell to her lips, then lifted again. "You're it for me, Seven. You're the one. I don't just want this moment with you. I want forever. Before we do this, I need to know that you understand what that means to a werewolf."

She frowned. Not this again. "Of course I understand. I was with Sentry my entire life, Lucas. I'm not stupid. You want to claim me as your mate. I *want* to be your mate or else I wouldn't be naked here underneath you. I've already told you that I love you—"

Whatever she'd been about to say was lost forever on a gasping moan as he thrust into her, not stopping until his hips touched hers and they were joined completely.

"You love me?" he growled against her lips.

"God, yes," she hissed, then groaned in frustration when he pinned her hips to the bed, refusing to let her move. "I already told you that."

"You never told me that."

Her brain was a little cloudy at the moment, but now that he mentioned it…

"Oh…well," she said. "I meant to. I had a whole speech planned earlier."

A speech she'd totally forgotten when she blurted out that she wanted to have sex with him. Ugh. She really had to get better at this whole communication thing.

"Say it now."

"I love you, Lucas."

His answering smile was like the dawn. "I love you too, beautiful."

His words brought tears to her eyes. He was so much more than she ever expected to have. She still wasn't sure she deserved him, but damn it, she also wasn't sure she cared anymore. He was a gift—her gift—and she wasn't going to give him up. Ever.

And then he began to move.

Lucas grabbed both her hands, pinned them at either side of her head, and threaded their fingers together. Seven wrapped her legs around his waist and held him tight as he drove into her, over and over again, slow but deep, while his mouth latched onto her neck, alternating between stinging bites and soothing swipes of his tongue.

He let go of one of her hands and slid his arm under her hips, pulling her tighter against him. She moaned as his pelvic bone ground against her clitoris. "Harder," she pleaded. "More."

He didn't hesitate to give her exactly what she wanted. Harder. Deeper. Faster. More. Again and again.

"You're mine," he whispered in her ear.

"Yes," she choked out. "And you're mine."

"Always."

And then his teeth sank into the curve of her shoulder. The claiming bite, she realized. The pain was sharp but fleeting, chased by white-hot pulses of pleasure starting right *there*—God, *yes*—where his mouth touched her skin, and surging through her entire body.

She came then, shuddering, driven over the edge by pain and pleasure, this climax a thousand times more powerful than the others he'd so generously given her. He followed her over the edge a moment later, thrusting into her one, two, three more times before going still, his body tensing above her.

Long, peaceful moments of silence passed as they clung to each other, breathing starting to return to normal, their mingled sweat drying, his forehead pressed to her shoulder, her hands stroking over the broad muscles of his back.

"So," she said when she caught her breath, "can I be claimed more than once? Like…a bunch more?"

His answering laughter shook the bed around them and sounded so purely happy that she couldn't help but smile in response.

"Darlin', I'll claim you ever night for the rest of our lives if that's what you want."

CHAPTER TWENTY-SEVEN

Seven woke up with half her body on top of Lucas and her face pressed into his neck. He had one arm thrown up over his face and the other wrapped around her, holding her against him, one large hand cupping her backside possessively.

She lifted her head and blinked in confusion at the shaft of sunlight piercing through the bedroom curtains and shining right in her face.

Something was off.

She never felt like this when she first woke up. Her body still pulsed and tingled in all the places Lucas had been last night, all the places he'd touched and kissed. Muscles she didn't even know she had ached deliciously.

That wasn't what was making her feel…different, she decided.

Seven sat up glanced down at Lucas and felt an immediate rush of tenderness. His face looked almost boyish first thing in the morning. All the hard lines of his features softened by sleep.

The illusion of boyishness abruptly evaporated when he shifted and the six-pack abs she'd traced with her tongue the night before rippled. And then there was the stubble covering his jaw that reminded her why she had whisker burn on her inner thighs.

A rush of something that definitely *wasn't* tenderness flooded her then.

But it wasn't lust that was making her feel different this morning, either. She'd felt plenty of that since he first kissed her.

Maybe the fact that she now had a mate was making her feel different.

No, that wasn't it, either. That was making her feel loved and cherished and safe for the first time in her life, but she'd felt that last night. What she was feeling now was something entirely new. Something she'd never experienced, not even when…

"That's it!" she blurted.

Lucas bolted upright, reaching instinctively for the gun he wasn't wearing.

"What's wrong?" He blinked blearily at her, his hair sticking up all over the place in a way that should've looked ridiculous, but definitely didn't. "What happened?"

"It's seven o'clock," she said, bouncing up to her knees on the mattress.

He glanced at the clock on the bedside table, then back at her, brow wrinkling. "Yeah…is that bad?"

"No! It's great! I slept! Like, *all night* I slept!"

He still looked confused. "I knew you were probably having a little trouble sleeping, but just how long has it been since you've slept all night, beautiful? Like, a full eight hours?"

"Pfffttt. Eight hours? Never. Until last night."

He thought about it for a moment, then finally seemed to catch up with the conversation. A grin of primitive, pure male satisfaction broke across his face. "So, you're saying that after one night with me, you're so worn out you can't help but sleep through the night for the first time ever?"

She knew he was joking, and she would've rolled her eyes at his arrogance if that wasn't *exactly* what she'd been thinking had happened. What other explanation was there? "That's what I'm saying."

His gaze dropped to her breasts for a moment before lifting to meet hers once again. He raised a brow at her. "Maybe if I wear you out some more, you'll be able go back to sleep for another few hours."

"Like a *nap*?" Was there anything in the world more decadent than a nap? She bounced a little on her knees, unable to contain her excitement. "I've never had a nap before! Do you really think that's possible?"

She squealed as he lunged for her, rolling her under him in one smooth motion like the predator he was.

"Only one way to find out," he growled.

As it turned out, he *was* able to wear Seven out to the point that a two-hour nap had been possible. It had taken four orgasms, but hey, he'd been more than happy to oblige. He was a giver, after all.

And now he had just one more thing he wanted to try and give her. But she clearly wasn't ready to take it just yet.

"Just give it a try. I'll be right there with you," he cajoled, tugging her gently into the bathroom.

"I don't like showers," she insisted for the tenth time, trying to dig her heels into the floor, and getting no help from the glossy marble.

Her words were casual, but the set of her jaw and the tension in her shoulders gave away her true feelings. She was terrified, and it ripped his heart out to see her like that. Seven deserved to be free of the past, and in his experience, the only way to do that was to face and overcome whatever scared you the most.

He knew Violet wouldn't agree with his methods, but damn it, he knew this woman better than she did. He had to try and help her.

"I know why you're afraid of the water," he told her gently.

For a moment, she looked like she might deny it. But eventually, she sighed and said, "And you think getting in that shower is going to help me forget?"

"No. Not forget. Move past." He cupped her jaw in one hand and lifted her chin so that she was looking him right in the eye. "If you get too scared at any point, we'll stop. I just want to try and help. Let me give you happy memories to replace the bad ones."

She swallowed hard. "I'm…afraid," she admitted.

"I know, beautiful," he murmured. "But I would never let anything bad happen to you. I mean it: if you get too scared, we'll stop. You just say the word. You're always safe with me. Always."

"Truth," she whispered.

He took a deep breath and pretended like her answer to what he was about to ask couldn't make or break him. "Do you trust me?"

She stared up at him so long and hard and with such intense concentration that he almost couldn't take it. But eventually, very quietly, she said, "Yes."

And damned if her trust wasn't the best gift he'd ever been given in his whole miserable life. It was humbling. He rested his forehead on hers and said, "You won't ever regret it."

"Just know that when I'm scared, I have a tendency to start hitting," she grumbled. "Just ask any guard at Midvale."

"I know," he said, his voice rumbling to the point that it sounded like a purr. "I remember. It was fucking hot."

Her snort turned into a moan as his mouth captured hers in a hungry, tongue-tangling kiss.

Not wanting to give her an opportunity to get away or think too much about what they were about to do, he lifted her up off the ground, forcing her to wrap her legs around his waist to keep her balance. Her arms went immediately around his neck as he inched them to the shower, his mouth never leaving hers, and turned on the water.

She trembled when he set her on her feet in the shower in front of him, her back to his chest. His body shielded her from the majority of the spray, but every time a stray drop hit her, she flinched like she'd been struck.

"Try to relax," he whispered in her ear. "You're so brave, beautiful. You can do this."

She turned her head and looked up at him with wide eyes that said she was only a few seconds away from throwing him to the ground and making a break for it. After what she'd been through, he could hardly blame her.

"Face forward and close your eyes," he said.

She did, albeit grudgingly, after a long, long stare-down. "I seriously doubt this is a scientifically proven method for curing aquaphobia," she grumbled.

"Oh, baby, I love it when you talk science to me. So hot," he teased.

She elbowed him in the gut. "I don't find you amusing."

Or so she said. But he could hear the laughter behind her words, even though she was clearly terrified.

God, he loved this woman.

He tipped her head back and shifted slightly so that the water was soaking her hair, but did his best to shield her face. Then he took his time working shampoo through the thick locks, slowly, thoroughly, paying particular attention to her scalp.

The longer he massaged her scalp, the more she started to relax. He could see the tightness start to leave her mouth, her neck, her shoulders, until finally she groaned and let her head fall back to rest on his shoulder.

He chuckled. "Good?"

Lucas decided to take her wordless moan as an affirmative. She didn't even protest when he sneakily moved them back further into the spray.

He shampooed, rinsed, and repeated twice more, and when he was done, she was almost completely under the spray. Her eyes were still closed, but she was practically limp in his arms.

He gave her hair a gentle tug so that she had to tip her head back a little, just enough that he could dip his own head down and touch his mouth to hers.

"You did it, beautiful," he whispered.

"Mmm."

She arched her back and pushed her ass back into his ever-present erection. It seemed he had no control over his body when she was around. Not that he really cared anymore.

And now that she wasn't scared anymore…

Lucas grabbed the soap and worked up a good lather before pressing her more firmly against him and gliding his wet, slick, soapy hands over her skin. *All* over her skin.

She moaned when he slid one hand between her legs and cupped her breast with the other. "Lucas," she murmured, throwing her head back against his shoulder again.

"Mmm. Nothing in this world sounds sexier than you moaning my name."

In less time than it took to relax her initially, she came hard, hips bucking, body jolting, until her legs gave out and he had to wrap an arm around her ribs to hold her up.

When she was steady on her feet again, he turned her around to face him, making sure his back was blocking the majority of the spray. She tipped her head back and looked up him, eyes glazed with lust. It was an exceptionally good look on her.

"And *that*," he told her, "is a shower."

"Wow," she breathed. "I've really been missing out."

"This is what I'm saying."

"I still don't think I could've done that on my own, though," she warned. "I'll probably need your help. You know, tomorrow. And probably…every day after that."

He grinned down at her when he realized she was teasing. She was starting to develop a decidedly quirky, wicked sense of humor as she settled into civilian life, and he fucking loved it.

"Well," he said, injecting as much seriousness into his voice as possible, "a lot of water gets wasted in America, which is bad for the environment. So, I think we owe it to ourselves, and to nature, of course, to share a shower every morning. And maybe every night, too."

She bit her lower lip before returning his grin as she grabbed the soap from the rack behind him and lathered up her hands. "I do like to live as green as possible."

Her soapy hands slid over his chest and down over his abs before grabbing his dick, which all but wept with joy at finally having her full attention.

"God bless green living," he said on a groan.

CHAPTER TWENTY-EIGHT

Two hours later, Lucas and Seven were sitting in Violet's waiting room, ready for Seven's standing weekly appointment.

They were also exceedingly clean.

Seven could definitely get used to taking showers with Lucas every morning. Particularly if they included a "happy ending," as he had called it.

And in her case, it had been a *very* happy ending.

What she wasn't really looking forward to was her upcoming conversation with Violet. She didn't expect Vi to be supportive of her relationship with Lucas. After all, Lucas had told her that part of the reason he'd put up so many emotional walls between them was because Violet had advised him about getting too involved with her.

She'd just have to convince her therapist that being with Lucas wasn't going to break her. If anything, it was fixing her. And if that didn't work…well, maybe she'd have to find another therapist.

Now that she had Lucas, there was *no one* that was going to take him from her. Just the thought of anyone trying made her want to hit something. The metal arms of her chair groaned under the weight of the death grip she had on them.

Lucas reached over, grabbed her hand, and brushed his lips over her knuckles. It was an easy, thoughtless gesture, as if they'd been together for decades instead of hours.

And just like that, her tension evaporated. Which was exactly the reaction he'd expected, she realized. He knew she was anxious, and he knew what would help her.

He was a miracle. And he was all *hers.*

"I love you," she said.

He winked at her. "I know."

She was about to reply when Violet's receptionist, Lexa, barreled into the room, phone to her ear.

Lexa was one of the most put-together people Seven had ever seen. She ran Violet's office with an iron fist. Seven had once seen Lexa—who was a tiny human, barely five-two, weighing no more than a hundred pounds—stand toe-to-toe with an irate vampire who'd shown up an hour late for his appointment and tell him he not only had to leave, but also pay a fine for the missed session. And when she narrowed her misty gray eyes on him, he backed down, apologized, and paid the fine. Seven had been impressed.

On a normal day, no matter how many calls she was fielding or how many clients were sitting in the waiting room, Lexa remained poised and professional, always looking perfect in her stylish pencil skirts, tailored button-down blouses, and humidity-impervious auburn curls.

But today obviously wasn't a normal day.

Lexa's hair was half up and half down, her clothes looked slept in, and she was wearing a haggard expression the likes of which Seven had never seen.

The whole *wrongness* of it raised a red flag in Seven's mind. A queasy feeling—the kind she only got when shit was about to hit the fan—hit her gut.

Lexa let out a frustrated growl and tossed her phone down on the reception desk.

Lucas leaned forward in his seat. "What's going on, Lex?"

She looked like she was barely holding back tears when her eyes lifted to his. "Lucas, I don't know what to do. Violet isn't here and she's not answering her phone. I haven't heard from her since yesterday afternoon when she left the office. She's missed three appointments."

To anyone on the outside listening in, they might not have been too concerned. After all, everyone missed appointments from time to time, right? Nope. Not Violet Marchand.

Seven's queasy feeling intensified.

Beside her, Lucas tensed. "Violet doesn't miss appointments," he murmured.

Lexa threw her hands up. "That's what I told the cops! In the eight years I've worked for her, Violet has never taken a sick day or missed an appointment. Hell, she's never so much as been *late* for an appointment. But the cops say a missing person's report can't even be filled out until she's been gone for twenty-four hours." She shook her head. "And she's not answering her home phone *or* her cell phone. I even tried calling her mom and her sister, and she's not with them. I'm telling you, Lucas, something is *wrong*. Like, *really* wrong."

"Do you have any idea where she was going when she left yesterday afternoon?" Seven asked.

Lexa immediately said, "She was going to the mall to pick out a new dress for her date."

Seven wrapped an arm around her middle and leaned forward to control the wave of nausea that now tore through her.

Lucas put his hand on her back. "Are you OK, beautiful? You look a little green."

"It's him. Her date," she said quietly. "He has her."

Lexa's gaze shot to hers. "How do you know that?"

Because of the acid that's currently eating a hole in my gut? "Gut feeling," she mumbled.

"I don't know," Lexa said. "She's been out with him a few times. If he was going to do anything to her, wouldn't he have done it before now?"

"Maybe, maybe not. Depends on what he was after. Maybe he was studying her." After all, that's what you did when you were targeting someone. You studied their every move, learned their every thought and desire. Seven should know. She'd had many, many targets back in her Sentry days.

And she'd be willing to bet that Violet had been targeted.

Her gut had never been wrong before. Why distrust it now?

Lucas rubbed her back soothingly and frowned at Lexa. "Who is this guy?"

Lexa sighed. "She was really tight-lipped about him. I don't know much."

"Anything you can remember might be helpful," Lucas told her.

"Well, he called here for her once and I answered, talked to him for a minute or two. He had an accent. It wasn't thick, but it definitely came out on certain words. Sounded like…Russian, maybe."

Lucas's hand still on Seven's back. "What else?"

Lexa rubbed her temples. "He came here to pick her up once, too. I only caught a glimpse of him as he was leaving, but I'd say he was about six-two, maybe one-eighty, dark hair. Kind of muscle-y."

Why did that physical description sound so familiar? Seven thought. Looking up to catch Lucas's eye, she saw the same question in his eyes.

"Oh," Lexa blurted, "he had a weird tattoo on his forearm. It looked like some kind of…bar code."

Seven's blood ran cold.

"Motherfucker," Lucas ground out. "I'm gonna find this guy and I'm gonna fuckin' kill him."

Lexa's eyes widened in alarm, but Seven ignored her. Grabbing Lucas's arm, she said, "You didn't tell me that the guy who shot at me had a bar code tattoo on his forearm."

His brow furrowed. "Why? Does that mean something to you?"

Her throat suddenly felt as dry as Sahara sand. "Yeah. I know who he is."

A muscle in Lucas's jaw jumped. "Who is he?"

Seven swallowed hard. "He's just like me."

CHAPTER TWENTY-NINE

Violet Marchand was an *excellent* ex-girlfriend.

She was, in her own humble opinion, the best, most understanding ex-girlfriend *ever*. When her high school boyfriend, the one she gave her V-card to, came out of the closet and dumped her for the captain of the football team? She didn't get angry and carve her name into the seats of his tricked-out F-150 pickup à la Carrie Underwood. No way. That would be uncivilized and would serve no one. Instead, she stepped aside gracefully and let them have their happiness.

When the happy couple had their commitment ceremony ten years later, they had her full blessing. She even did a lovely poetry reading at their reception.

When her college boyfriend cheated on her with her roommate, she didn't cause any drama for them. She quietly moved out and never looked back.

Her sister was marrying Violet's grad school boyfriend in a few months, too. No hard feelings. She'd already agreed to be matron of honor. And in all honesty, he'd always been kind of a pompous douchebag, anyway. Bullet dodged, she supposed, even if he was still going to be her brother-in-law.

Did she hold onto a grudge when she discovered Lucas had a thing for Harper? Heck no. Onward and upward, that was her motto. Lucas wasn't the right man for her. Her Prince Charming would arrive eventually.

But something told her that her excellent ex-girlfriend status was about to be seriously tested by her latest mistake.

If he let her live, that is.

Vi really should've realized something was wrong with Nik—Nikolai Aleyev—long ago. He was just too…perfect. Gentlemanly, attentive, not too forward, stunningly gorgeous, interested in her work, insanely gorgeous, funny in a desert-dry kind of way (did she mention he was sex-on-a-stick crazy-gorgeous?)…that kind of guy had never shown any interest in her before.

But she'd had hope. Hope that maybe *this* man was the reason none of her other relationships had worked out. Hope that *this* man was The One.

And, God, hope was addictive. Allow just a little of it to creep into your heart and before long, you'll find yourself tranquilized and zip-tied to a chair in an abandoned machine shop.

Or at least, that was Vi's current experience.

"Fucking hope," she muttered.

Vi closed her eyes and took a few steadying breaths as she struggled to remember exactly what had happened the night before.

She'd met Nik at her favorite Mexican restaurant, El Padre's, because they had the best salsa anywhere within a forty-mile radius of Whispering Hope and served burritos as big as her head. And what could be better than a warm, spicy burrito with…

Focus, she chastised herself.

Nik had arrived before her, and had a margarita waiting for her. Margaritas were her favorite. At the time, she'd thought, *oh, how sweet. He remembers me ordering a margarita on our first date and me telling him how much I enjoyed them.* He'd even remembered that she preferred the bartender to line the rim with sugar instead of salt. But now she realized that what she'd taken as *sweet* was really quite strategic.

It was the perfect opportunity to slip drugs into her drink without her knowledge.

Rule number one of frat parties: never let your drink out of your sight.

It'd been her damn motto in college. She let out a harsh laugh. *Just look at me now.*

At some point during their meal (after the burrito, before cinnamon churros), Vi remembered getting tired. Not the regular kind of I-stayed-up-a-little-too-late-reading-the-night-before tired she was used to experiencing, but a kind of bone-deep fatigue that made her eyelids so heavy she doubted her ability to drive herself home. It was at that point that Nik checked his watch and said he needed to leave. He said he'd walk her to her car.

She remembered thinking that she liked that. He didn't ask if she wanted him to walk her to her car like her last boyfriend had. Like it'd be an imposition, but he'd do it if he had to. No, not Nik. Nik pretty much insisted he walk her to her car. So manly and protective.

She now knew *that too* had been strategic.

On their way to the car, he'd put his hand on the small of her back, which sent heat waves up and down her spine. She hadn't wanted him to put her in her car and leave. She wanted him to run those big, warm, work-roughened hands all over her body. At that point she'd known that if he asked, she was going home with him. They hadn't even kissed yet, but she was more than willing to put out on their fourth date.

"Stupid," she hissed, squirming in the chair, trying to break the zip ties at her wrists and ankles. "So fucking stupid."

The ties didn't budge, except to cut into the delicate skin of her wrists. Awesome, she thought as she felt a trickle of blood ease from her torn wrist up into the sleeve of her slinky black dress.

Yet another indignity. She'd actually purchased a new outfit for this date. A beautiful, silk outfit fit for a, well, kidnapping, as it turned out. And the best part? It had cost her as much as a month's rent. So, if by some miracle she actually lived through this day, she'd most likely spend the next month eating ramen noodles so she could afford the rent on her apartment and office building.

But if that's where the indignities ended, she could survive it. What really irked her, made her wish she could disappear in a puff of misery, was the kiss.

They'd been on their way to her car when her heel slipped out from under her. Nik had caught her before she could fall and scooped her up into his arms, cradling her against his chest.

"It's OK, *kotehok*," he whispered in a soothing voice. "I've got you."

She had no idea what *kotehok* meant, but the way his deep, slightly accented voice caressed the word was hot as hell. Honestly, he could probably call her whatever he wanted in that voice and she'd be OK with it.

Even as a wave of dizziness washed over her, she remembered wrapping her arms around his neck, and being acutely aware of just how much of her body was touching his. He was so warm—hot even—despite the chill in the air, and his skin smelled *so* good. Like laundry detergent and some kind of masculine soap, not expensive cologne or aftershave. He was *real* and so strong and solid, and in that moment, she wanted nothing more than his mouth on hers.

So, in her hazy mind, lifting her head and pressing her lips to his seemed like a perfectly reasonable move.

He stumbled to a stop and went perfectly still for a moment, stunned, muscles tightly coiled. But just when she was starting to feel embarrassed for being so forward, he recovered and kissed her back. And…wow. What a kiss it was.

Kissing Nik was nothing like kissing any of her exes. He tasted warm and sweet, like the wine he'd had with dinner, which had reminded her that she probably tasted like a giant burrito. Probably not at all sexy, but he hadn't seemed to mind. He'd growled low in his throat as their tongues tangled, and his hands tightened on her reflexively.

Vi remembered moaning and shifting in his arms, pressing herself against him tighter, feeling like she wanted to crawl inside him. Like she'd never get close enough. He'd responded by deepening the kiss.

It hadn't been a movie-perfect kiss—it was too hot and fast and wild for that—but it was *so* much better than any kiss she'd ever had, so *intimate*. For the first time in, well, *way* too long, Vi actually felt *connected* to someone. It had felt like a lost part of herself had just clicked back into place, making her whole once again.

"Get a room!" someone shouted, completely ruining the moment.

Nik pulled back and rested his forehead on hers, muttering something under his breath in Russian.

That's when her head was suddenly too heavy to hold up anymore. A moment later, Nik tucked her into the passenger seat of her car and buckled her belt.

When he climbed into the driver's seat and started the car, he said, "Just rest, *kotehok*. I'm not going to hurt you. Everything will be just fine."

That's when she'd finally figured it out. Nik had drugged her and was taking her somewhere.

He was taking her *here*, as it turned out. She glanced around ruefully. Wherever the fuck *here* was.

OK, Marchand, time to get serious. Stop feeling sorry for yourself and figure out how you're going to get out of this.

Now that her mind was clear and all the details of the previous day had fallen back into place, she made note of her surroundings.

The warehouse was huge, probably the size of a football field. Grime—either from decades of use or years of abandonment, she couldn't be sure which—coated every flat surface. Dust motes in the air tickled her sinuses, reminding her that she'd forgotten to take a

Claritin before her date. Her seasonal allergies were a bitch this time of year.

Sunlight flooded in through the huge, half-busted out windows that were situated all around the room, high up by the ceiling, which was nearly as tall as the space was long. Getting to those windows wouldn't be easy, even if she wasn't tied to a chair.

Rusted-out machinery she couldn't even begin to identify cluttered the space. Maybe, if she could get to some of it, she could break off a piece to use as a weapon.

But just like the windows, getting to them wasn't going to be easy with the whole *tied to a chair* thing happening.

Getting out of the chair was going to have to be her number-one priority. On TV, the way to get out of being tied to a chair was to tip it over and break it. She was pretty sure she'd seen Sydney Bristow on *Alias* do that very thing a time or two.

Of course, she was no Sydney Bristow. She could just as easily tip her chair over, crack her head open on the dirty cement floor, and bleed to death before anyone even knew she was here. That certainly wasn't a very appealing idea.

But what choice did she have? Sit here and wait for Nik to come back? Who the hell knew what *he* had in store for her? For all she knew, he was planning to make her part of a woman suit he was stitching in his basement out of human skin, or wear her head around like a hat.

Damn you, Silence of the Lambs *for putting shit like that in my head!*

No, she had to get out of here before that happened.

Before she could analyze and overthink it too much (as she was prone to do), she closed her eyes, took a deep breath, and threw all her weight to one side as hard as she could.

Every muscle in her body tightened, anticipating how much it was going to hurt to hit that concrete.

But the pain never came.

When she opened her eyes, her chair was once again upright, and she was eye-to-eye with her kidnapper.

The look he gave her was full of pity.

"I'm sorry, *kotehok*," he said in that same soothing voice that had once turned her on. Now it just pissed her off. "I can't let you do that. I'm afraid you'll need to stay with me for a bit longer."

Violet closed her eyes again and swallowed hard, wondering if *a bit longer* was a euphemism for *until death do us part*. The death being hers, of course.

CHAPTER THIRTY

A few hours later, Seven, Lucas, Harper, Riddick, Benny, Mischa, and Hunter huddled around the conference room table at Harper Hall Investigations, trying to figure out what the hell was going on.

Lucas shoved his hands through his hair in frustration. "How can we not know where he's holding her?" He threw Harper a sharp look. "You're a psychic, for God's sake. Can't you figure it out?"

The look she lobbed back at him was equally sharp. "Yeah, sure. Why didn't I think of that? I'll just look into my crystal ball and…oh, wait. My crystal ball is broken!" Her hands flew to her cheeks like Macaulay Culkin in *Home Alone*. "What'll we do now?"

He sighed. Yeah, he supposed he deserved that. He knew her power didn't exactly work that way. Without something of the kidnapper's to touch, Harper's ability would do precious little to help them find Vi. But, in a desperate situation, reason often went right out the window.

Mischa shook her head, but didn't look up from the Sentry file—which looked about a foot thick—she was digging through. "I don't think sarcasm will help us in this situation, Harper."

She crossed her arms over her chest. "Can't hurt, either," she grumbled.

Riddick stood up, moved behind his wife's chair and laid his hands on her shoulders. To Seven, he said, "Are you sure about his designation, sweetheart?"

"Yes," she answered quietly. "The only cleaner I knew who had a barcode on his forearm was designated 654590. He fit the description of the man Violet's been dating."

Seven was sitting next to Lucas with one arm wrapped around her stomach while her other hand was massaging her temple. She was the absolutely picture of guilt.

Well, fuck that, Lucas thought.

Lucas yanked her up out of her chair and pulled her down onto his lap, wrapping his arms around her. "It's not your fault," he whispered in her ear before pressing a kiss to her temple. "We'll get her back."

She looked down at him for a moment like she might argue, but eventually, she nodded. He let out the breath he didn't realize he'd been holding when she wrapped her arms around him and pressed her face into his neck.

This is what coming home feels like, he realized. He'd wanted this for *so* long, and now, despite everything that was going on, *home* had finally fallen right into his lap. Quite literally, in fact.

And God help anyone or anything who tried to take her from him.

Lucas tightened his hold on Seven and let one of his hands drift up to tangle in her hair. She responded by wiggling even closer and letting out a deep, satisfied sigh. God, she felt *so* good. Smelled great, too. When this was all over and they had Vi back, the first he was going to do was take her home, toss her on the bed and not let her up again until…

Benny cleared his throat. Loudly.

When Lucas looked up and met his gaze, Benny said, "EHO, man."

"What's EHO?"

"Eye hard on," Harper explained, gesturing to his eyes, which he was sure were blazing yellow, as they always did when he was angry, particularly stressed, or…turned on.

Well, shit.

Seven pulled back to see, and her softly whispered, "Wow, that looks even prettier in the daylight" did absolutely nothing to help the situation.

And that's when he realized all work had stopped and he had everyone's full attention.

Well…double shit.

Hunter's expression remained politely impassive, but his wife looked like she was trying so hard to keep a laugh in that she might hurt herself. Harper gave him a wide smile and a not-at-all subtle thumbs up, while Benny hid a laugh—also not discreet—behind a cough.

Meanwhile, Riddick was looking at him in a cold, narrow-eyed, calculating way that made Lucas's skin crawl. If he had to guess, he'd say Riddick was determining the most efficient way to separate his limbs from his body.

Lucas shrugged it all off, deciding that "well, fuck it" was going to be his new mantra. After all, that mantra was at least partially responsible for getting him here and getting this beautiful woman in his arms.

Mischa turned her attention back to the file and whistled. "Man, this dude has not had an easy life."

Lucas frowned at her. "Can't say I feel too sorry for him, seeing as he's kidnapped our friend. None of us has had a particularly easy life and we haven't kidnapped or shot at anyone."

"No, I know that," Mischa said. "But…still."

"What's his sob story?" Harper asked. "Maybe it'll help us figure out why he'd take Vi and try and kill Seven."

Mischa flipped through a couple more pages in the file. "Well, he was born in Russia. Mother and father were part of a Bratva, a Russian mafia family."

"Like Viggo Mortenson in *Eastern Promises*?" Harper asked.

Lucas shook his head. Harper's ability to relate any situation to television and movies was astounding. Not at all helpful, but astounding nonetheless. Playing Six Degrees of Kevin Bacon with her was a real learning experience.

Mischa blinked at her. "Yeah, sure," she said, clearly having no idea what Harper was talking about.

"Ooohhh, Naomi Watts was so hot in that," Benny said.

And Benny's ability to reduce any story down to the presence of hot women was, well, disturbing, really, and no more useful than Harper's contributions to the conversation.

"As I was saying," Mischa said in a tone as dry as day-old bread, "His family wanted out. Bratva's aren't real big on letting people out, so they killed them. Our guy had no other family and was sent to an orphanage when he was only a few years old. That's where he got the bar code."

Harper's nose wrinkled up. "They *branded* him at an orphanage? I thought orphanages were run by nuns and missionaries and shit. You know, by people who actually want to *help* kids. What the fuck?"

"It's not uncommon in some parts of the world," Hunter murmured. "Especially not in orphanages that are really just a front for criminals looking to sell black market babies."

"Ugh," Benny muttered. "The world is just a fucking hotbed of sicko activity, isn't it?"

Truer words were never spoken.

"So, he was sold to Sentry?" Seven asked. "Like me?"

Lucas felt his jaw clench involuntarily. Hearing a word like "sold" in relation to the woman he loved made him feel homicidal.

"Yes," Mischa said. "But it was much harder for him than it was for you."

Lucas bristled at that. "What the hell, Mischa? She hasn't had one *easy* thing in her life. I'm thinking your definition of *easy* must be fairly well fucked up."

"You'll watch your tone with my wife," Hunter snapped.

The "or I'll rip out your still-beating heart" was implied, not stated. Hunter was a vampire of few words, but he'd never really had any trouble making his feelings known.

Before Lucas could say anything to dig a deeper hole for himself, Seven pressed a kiss to his temple and leaned back to look him in the eye. His ire evaporated when she smiled at him. She was telling him, without saying a word, that she appreciated his support, but it was unnecessary.

Apparently Seven and Hunter subscribed to the same school of thought when it came to communication. Minimalists, both of them.

"Sorry, Mischa," Lucas mumbled.

Mischa waved off his apology. "No worries. What I was trying to say is that, Seven, you were raised in the program. You didn't really know anything else. So, you were pretty much the perfect Sentry employee. You took to their way of doing things easily. But our guy? He remembered what it was like to be in a family and be loved. He fought them every step of the way. Apparently, he was sent for reprogramming several times."

"That can't be good thing," Benny said, then gave an exaggerated shudder.

"It's not," Mischa murmured. "It pretty much amounted to torture and brainwashing to break him."

Lucas felt a shiver run through Seven, and he knew she was most likely remembering what torture and having someone try to break her felt like. He tightened his hold on her, hoping he could comfort her with his nearness like she comforted him.

Benny elbowed Harper and stage-whispered, "Is it wrong that I feel a little sorry for the kidnapper-slash-attempted murderer?"

Harper crossed her arms over her chest. "Well I do. God, I hate it when the bad guys make me feel sorry for them. That's just not right."

Riddick rolled his eyes. "I don't care if they did all that to him *and* drowned his puppy. He kidnapped Vi and tried to kill my sister, so I don't feel even a little bit sorry for the motherfucker. I say we find him and kill him."

Now *there* was a plan Lucas could get behind. Who would've thought he'd end up agreeing with *Riddick* about anything?

Benny leaned over to Harper again. "You don't really think they drowned his puppy, do you?"

She shrugged. "Maybe. Seems like something the Russian mafia or the sicko orphan-branding baby-sellers would do, you know?"

Benny nodded. "Word."

"Is he…like me?" Seven asked quietly.

Lucas could've kissed her for bringing the conversation back on track and howled in outrage at the same time, because he heard the sympathy in her voice. She was feeling sorry for the dude who tried to kill her just like Harper and Benny were. If she had her way, Riddick's "find him and kill him" plan—and had he mentioned how much he *loved* that plan?—was definitely in danger.

Mischa sighed. "I'm guessing so. It would certainly explain his record with Sentry. He was faster, stronger, and smarter than the other cleaners, just like you were. He was able to withstand reprogramming *four times* before breaking. Most didn't survive the first."

"Which would mean that when we find him," Hunter said carefully, "his fate is in the hands of the Vampire Council, not the human police."

Lucas and Riddick let out disgusted sighs in stereo. The "find him and kill him" plan was definitely off. Hunter was all about fair trials and unbiased evaluations before any actions were taken against a member of the paranormal community. Which was usually fine. It just wasn't fine *today*.

Not when his wolf was ready to hunt.

"Oh!" Mischa cried out. "Here we go! Well, hello there, Nikolai Aleyev, otherwise known as Sentry cleaner designation 654590!"

And with a flourish, she pulled a picture out of the file and slapped it down in the middle of the table.

Finally, Lucas thought. Something they could use. He could scan this, run it through the federal database, see if facial recognition software could help them figure out what identity this guy might be using and where he might be. Then they could—

"Motherfucker!" Harper shouted, grabbing the photo off the table. "I know this guy!"

Riddick snatched the picture from her hand and scowled at it. "How do you know him? Is he a client or something? Someone you knew from Sentry?"

She let out a humorless laugh. "I wish. It's much worse than that."

A look crossed Harper's face that Lucas had never seen on her before. She looked embarrassed.

Eventually, after a full minute of everyone watching her, waiting, she admitted, rather sheepishly, "I rented him the basement apartment a few months ago."

Jesus Christ. He'd been right under their noses—quite literally—all along. "Son of a bitch!" Lucas blurted, slamming his hand down on the conference room table.

Harper let out a weak chuckle and gave the universal "Oops, my bad" shoulder shrug. "I know, right? I swear to God, he seemed really normal."

"Babe," Riddick said, shaking his head. "Did you run a background check?"

"I didn't have to!" she said defensively. "I had my mother talk to him. She said he was a decent guy. Just…"

"Just what?" Lucas asked through gritted teeth.

Harper bit into her thumbnail and muttered, "She said he was a little emotionally…*off*, OK? She didn't have much more to go on than that, but I didn't think it was important because she said he was a decent guy! He called her ma'am, walked her to her car, and everything!"

"What did you *think 'a little emotionally off'* meant?" Mischa asked, incredulous.

"I don't know. That he liked to dress up as a Smurf on the weekends and let German octogenarians spank him?" She threw her hands up in frustration. "I don't know! Hell, '*a little emotionally off*' could apply to any of us."

Lucas had no reply to that. Couldn't have come up with a reply if his life depended on it. Fortunately, Hunter put the conversation back on the rails. He said, "Let's go check out his apartment. Harper, maybe you can pick up a vision from something of his. If not, Lucas, maybe you can trail him by scent."

"Fucking finally," Riddick grumbled. "A *plan*."

Truer words, my monosyllabic douchebag friend. Truer words.

As they all piled into the elevator, Benny asked Harper, "Um…that bit about German old people spanking dudes dressed like Smurfs…you were just making that up, right? That's not really a *thing*, is it?"

The look she shot him in response had them all suppressing a shudder.

Yep. So, pretty much all they'd established today is that Harper didn't do thorough background checks before renting out parts of her building, and the world was a fucking hotbed of sicko activity.

Perfect. At least the day hadn't been a total waste.

CHAPTER THIRTY-ONE

Every bit of hostage negotiator training she'd ever had flew right out of Vi's head as Nik knelt in front of her. Not that it really mattered. It's not like any of the police department's training covered what to do when *you* were the hostage.

"Why are you doing this?" she asked, silently cursing her voice for trembling.

He looked her right in the eye, not an ounce of shiftiness or nervousness in his countenance—damn him—and said, "I need information about one of your patients."

"I'm bound by doctor-patient confidentiality," she answered on autopilot.

"I understand. But if one of your patients planned to hurt or kill someone, that doctor-patient confidentiality doesn't apply. You'd be bound to tell the authorities, yes? Think of me as the authorities in this case."

Damn him for sounding so reasonable. "If you suspected one of my patients of…wrongdoing why didn't you just tell me in the first place? Why go through with the charade of dating me?" *Of making me feel like a fool. Of making me actually believe you were a good guy, damn it.* The *good guy.*

He at least had the grace to look a little ashamed of himself this time. "I never intended to lead you on or hurt you in any way, Violet."

In the name of self-preservation, there were just a few things she was going to need to ignore, Violet decided. First of all, she was just going to have to ignore the way his thick, dark, slightly unruly hair fell across his brow while he spoke to her, and the way her fingers itched to smooth it back.

Stupid, self-destructive fingers.

The second thing she refused to notice was the way his rough, grumbly, lightly accented voice caressed each syllable of her name. And if she *was* to ever notice such a thing—against her will, of course—she would absolutely *not* find it sexy. Nope. Not. At. All. Sexy.

Finally, she was just going to have to ignore the sincerity shining in his pale green eyes when he said he'd never intended to hurt her. Because frankly, as she sat here *tied to a chair*, the words just didn't ring true, no matter how beautifully they'd been delivered.

"And I couldn't entirely rule out that you might be the intended target," he added. "I had to make sure, and this was the only way I knew to get close to you."

And get close he had. Close enough that she'd had her tongue down his throat.

Ugh. Yet another thing she was going to have to ignore: the fact that she'd kissed this man. And worst of all, she'd loved it and wanted more. Way more. Like, *naked* more.

"So, you think one of my patients could be trying to kill me," she said, lowering her gaze and carefully erasing any hint of *I don't believe you, you freak* show from her voice.

Sadly, it wasn't a terribly farfetched theory. Her patients ranged in mental stability from docile to psychotic and everything in between.

But still, the fact that she was here, *tied to a chair*, had her seriously doubting his truthfulness.

When he didn't answer her question, she glanced up and found that he was staring at her bound hands, frowning. She followed his gaze to a small patch of raw skin on her wrist—*note to self: pulling against zip ties is a painful waste of effort*—and a little trickle of blood that had run down to her hands, staining her nailbeds an unsightly pink. If she lived through this, she'd definitely need a new manicure.

Nik muttered a harsh-sounding Russian word and stood up. When he pulled a switchblade out of his back pocket and raised it, Vi wanted to scream, but terror practically closed her throat up and all she managed to get out was a pathetic squeak as she flinched and brought her bound hands up to protect her face.

After a moment of not feeling a blade sliding between her ribs to pierce her heart, Vi peeked through her fingers to find Nik looking down at her with an unfathomable expression, hands—and the knife—raised.

"I won't hurt you, *kotehok*," he murmured in that grumbly baritone of his. "You have my word. I cut ties at your wrists, yes?"

His accent was thicker, she noticed. And he was dropping articles in his speech, saying "cut ties" instead of "cut *the* ties," which she'd never known him to do before. Vi couldn't help but wonder if the emotion she saw but couldn't quite identify in his eyes was responsible. Maybe that emotion was something she could use to her advantage to escape.

Or maybe that emotion was what was eventually going to get her killed.

Vi swallowed hard and lifted her hands to him, praying she wasn't reading too much into his seemingly sincere offer.

"What does *kotehok* mean?" she asked.

One corner of his mouth quirked up as he leaned in and took both her wrists in one of his hands. "In English it means kitten."

She frowned, ignoring how wonderful his strong, callused fingers felt on her cold skin and how he smelled like sunshine-dried laundry. "Because I'm fluffy and harmless?"

His smile grew and a dimple—goddamn him, a *dimple*!—carved into his cheek. "Because you're sweet but have sharp claws when you want to use them, and because I've wanted to make you purr ever since I first saw you."

Her breath lodged in her throat and she couldn't have worked up a decent reply if her life depended on it. He was flirting with her! Her kidnapper was *flirting* with her. How in the hell was she supposed to respond to *that*?

Well, she certainly couldn't admit that before he drugged her and *tied her to a chair* she'd been about five minutes away from begging him to take her to a bed—or a couch, or a shower, or a wall, or, well, pretty much anywhere—and make her purr.

It had been a really, really long time since she'd last…purred.

His smile faded when she didn't reply. He cleared his throat. "My apologies," he mumbled. "That was inappropriate."

Well, this just got more and more confusing. So, Nik was a polite kidnapper who'd promised not to hurt her, and made her nipples go on high alert whenever he was in the same room with her.

My life is so fucked up.

She sighed as he sliced through the ties at her wrists. "Just tell me what's going on, Nik. Who did you think might be trying to kill me?"

Vi winced as he grabbed a bottle of water and wet her sore wrists, then dabbed gently—much more gently than she'd expect from a man his size—at the abraded skin with a clean T-shirt he'd pulled from his duffel bag. (Or, his serial killer go-bag, as she'd been thinking of it since she woke up.)

"Sentry cleaner designation 754821," he eventually answered, eyes still cast down on the task of cleaning up her wrists and rubbing some circulation back into her icy fingers.

"Seven? You thought *Seven* was trying to kill me?" Of all the patients who could be trying to kill her, Seven was last on her list. Vi shook her head. "No. She's making tremendous progress. She wouldn't do anything to jeopardize that."

"The only *progress* Sentry cleaners make is getting close to their targets and eliminating them," he said, voice going hard for the first time in, well, *ever*. "If the target isn't you, there are many other possibilities. The shifter, the halfer, the vampires, the slayer, the psychic…" he paused, throwing his hands up in frustration. "I can't tell which one—or ones—she's after."

So he'd been watching Seven. He'd seen her with Lucas, Benny, Mischa, Hunter, Riddick, and Harper. Which meant her nipples went on high alert for a guy who was a drink-drugger, a kidnapper, *and* a stalker.

And if he was all those things, he probably…oh, God. "You were the one who tried to kill her that night in the alley, weren't you?"

Please say no. Please say no. Please say no.

His short nod made her stomach sink down to the pointed toes of her sleek black Louboutins. "I acted without thought and I failed," he said. "I won't do it again."

His first instinct, probably because of his training, had just been to take her out. But he now he wanted more information about her and her plans. So that…he could more be a more efficient assassin?

She swallowed hard. "Seven doesn't want to kill anyone. "Riddick and Harper are her family. The others you saw her with are her friends. She's just trying to build a life for herself."

The look he gave her was dangerously close to pity. "Cleaners don't have family and they certainly don't have friends. Cleaners hunt. Kill. It's all they know."

He sounded so sure of that, she had to wonder… "How do you know so much about cleaners?"

So many emotions filtered through his eyes. Pain, shame, anger, frustration. He was usually so calm, so in control. And right now? He was anything but. That answered her question more clearly than words ever could.

"You were a cleaner like Seven, weren't you, Nik?" she asked quietly.

He lowered his head and his hands went to his hips, the very picture of frustrated alpha male. But he didn't answer her. Instead, he took a deep breath and gestured to the ties at her ankles. "If I cut those," he said, his voice even lower and more…grumbly than usual, "can I trust you to *not* try and run away?"

Nope. Not even a little bit. "Yes."

Nik laughed, but it was the most humorless, world-weary laugh she'd ever heard. "You're lying. Not that I blame you. But I'm sorry, *kotehok*. I can't risk it. This isn't a good neighborhood. Having you wandering around out there looking for help…it's just not safe."

Being out *there* wasn't safe, but being in *here*, with the drink-drugging, kidnapping, stalking, nipple-hardener who wanted her patient dead was somehow *better* for her well-being? That hardly seemed possible.

And second of all…how did he know she was lying? She was a *great* liar. No one could ever tell when she was lying. What made him so different?

Vi licked her lips nervously. "So, I guess we're at a stalemate. I can't tell you what you want to know about Seven. What do we do now?"

She lifted her eyes to his and noticed his gaze locked on her mouth. Her heart threatened to pound its way out of her chest as her brain tripped into *OhmyGodOhmyGodOhmyGod* territory. Was he remembering their kiss? Was he as affected by her as she was by him? Shit! That couldn't be good! Wait…could it?

Slowly his eyes lifted and met hers again. The normal pale green she was used to seeing had gone smoky and dark with need. She couldn't have looked away at that moment if the National Guard knocked the door down to rescue her.

"I'll call her here on your phone and ask her myself," he eventually said. "She'll come for you, yes?"

Well, that didn't sound so bad. Maybe she hadn't been so terribly wrong about him after all. Maybe he wasn't such a bad guy. "Then what?"

"When I know who her target is?"

"Yes. What then?"

"Then you can go home."

She let out a deep breath as relief washed over in waves. *Thank you, Jesus. Thank you for not crushing my hopes this time.*

Then he added, "And then I kill her."

Vi just blinked at him for a moment, sure she'd misunderstood. When it became clear she hadn't, she closed her eyes and let her chin hit her chest.

"Fucking hope," she muttered.

CHAPTER THIRTY-TWO

The apartment where 654590—no, Nikolai—lived was exactly what Seven expected. It reminded her of every place she'd ever stayed while working on assignment for Sentry.

One overstuffed brown leather sofa, a banged-up dinette set with a pair of mismatched chairs, and a king-size mattress were the only pieces of furniture in the place. No pictures, no television, nothing decorative or personal of any kind.

Beyond that, the place was so clean, smelling not-so faintly of bleach, that Seven suspected he wiped everything down for fingerprints daily. He'd be able to up and leave this place at a moment's notice, and would do just that when the job was done.

When she was dead, Seven assumed.

Knowing that a fellow cleaner, one who was most likely also a *dhampyre*, was trying to kill her should probably upset Seven more than it did, or at least make her hate the guy. But oddly enough, she found that she just felt…sorry for Nikolai.

Seven *understood* him. Felt for him a way that few could, she would imagine. He was doing a job. The job he'd been trained to do.

A job he'd been brainwashed and tortured into doing.

It was pretty hard to hate a guy who, at heart, wasn't really all that different from Seven herself.

Lucas clearly didn't see it that way, though.

"Anything yet?" he grumbled, frustration and anger rolling off him in shimmering waves.

Harper pursed her lips and shot him a glare. "Premonitions aren't like a lunch special, Lucas. I can't always just *order* one for myself. Sometimes it doesn't come easy. It'll happen when it happens."

Lucas exhaled sharply. "We don't have time for this."

Benny snorted as he leaned a shoulder against the doorjamb. "And what should we do instead? Run up and down the street yelling 'Marco!' and hoping Vi gives us a 'Polo!' in return? Good plan, dude."

Seven grabbed Lucas's hand when he took a menacing step toward Benny. "He's right," she said quietly. "Our best hope is Harper at this point."

Lucas exhaled sharply, but thankfully, seemed to realize the truth in her words. Hunter and Mischa had returned to Council headquarters to see if they could dig up anything additional in the old records, but if Nikolai was as good at his job as Seven had been at hers, she'd be willing to bet he'd long ago broken from any patterns that might lead them to Violet.

And given the overly clean smell of the apartment, there was likely no way Lucas could pick up so much as a hint of Nikolai's scent for tracking purposes. At this point, if Harper couldn't use her psychic ability to find them, they were screwed. If Nikolai didn't want to be found, he wouldn't be.

Riddick came out of the bedroom and handed a black T-shirt to Harper. "This was in the closet. Maybe it'll help."

While she smiled at him and shifted the shirt from one hand to the other, Riddick motioned for them to follow him back into the bedroom. “I also found this,” he said, gesturing to the closet.

“Son of a bitch,” Lucas muttered.

Yeah, that about covered it, Seven thought as she took in some of the most thorough surveillance work she’d ever seen.

On the back of the closet door were pictures. Pictures of her with Lucas, Benny, Riddick, Harper...hundreds of pictures. There were enough of them to suggest Nikolai had been watching her every minute of every day since she’d been released from Midvale. Until…

Somewhere along the line, the focus of his surveillance seemed to shift to Vi. He must’ve assumed he could get to Seven through Vi. And he’d been right, apparently.

They were all stunned into silence except for Harper, who tossed the shirt over her shoulder and clapped her hands like a little kid on Christmas morning. “Ooohhh yeah,” she said, “Now *that’s* what I’m talking about. Come to momma.”

Without another word, she slapped her palms on the door and closed her eyes, brow furrowing in concentration.

The next four or five minutes felt like days as they watched Harper’s facial expressions change as visions flooded her. Anger, sadness, confusion…they flitted across her face quickly, like channels on TV with someone absentmindedly clicking a heavy finger on the remote.

When she finally pulled her shaking hands away from the door, Harper stumbled, clearly exhausted from channeling so much power. After so many training sessions with Hunter, Seven knew the feeling. Riddick moved faster than Seven had ever seen to grab his wife and scoop her up in his arms.

"What did you see?" Lucas and Benny asked in stereo, then frowned at each other.

"Give her a fucking minute," Riddick growled.

Harper patted his chest and shook her head. "No, I'm fine. It was just…a lot to take in."

Seven glanced back at the photos, noticing something odd. "Do the photos of Violet seem…different than the photos of me?"

Lucas frowned. "Different how?"

Benny squinted at them. "The pictures of Seven are wide shots. Serious surveillance-type shit to get an idea of background, time, and location. The ones of Dr. Hot Stuff start out like that, but then they turn into close-ups. They get kinda…I dunno…*Fatal Attraction*, maybe? Obsessive-like?"

Everyone turned to look at him in stunned silence. He eventually ran a finger under his collar nervously and said, "What? I can't be good for more than just comic relief and eye candy every now and then? I got a brain, you know. I'm capable of saying insightful shit."

Harper was the first to find her tongue. "Benny's pretty much dead-on. Our guy is definitely into Vi in a *big* way. He's all twisted up over the idea of her being in danger."

Lucas scoffed. "So he kidnapped her to protect her? What a bunch of bullshit."

"Maybe," Harper said, "but that's what he was thinking. He thinks Seven's either trying to carry out a mission, or that she's going to go on some kind of rogue killing spree. He doesn't want to take her out until he knows who her target is, though. If Seven's on a legit mission, he intends to complete it once she's dead."

He was carrying out the *final* mission. The one all cleaners had been instructed to carry out should Sentry ever fall. It's what she would do if she was him.

"We're the last two cleaners," Seven whispered. "Aren't we? He killed the others."

Harper nodded. "There were five others left, other than you two. He killed them while you were in Midvale." She shuddered. "From what I saw? They needed to be killed. Without Sentry's guidance, they were out of control. Like *Dexter*, only without Harry's code to guide him."

"Shit, I miss that show," Benny murmured sadly.

Seven had no idea who Harry and Dexter were, but she overlooked it. She was getting used to only understanding about half of what Harper said at any given time. It was usually enough. "Did you get any idea of where he might be keeping her?"

"Not really. I mostly saw Nikolai. What Sentry did to him to try and break him?" Harper shook her head. "It's a miracle he has any functioning brain cells left. He's definitely a *dhampyre*, because no human could've taken that."

Lucas shoved a hand through his hair. "Something about this isn't adding up. So, he killed the other cleaners because that was part of the Sentry plan, right? If Sentry was to shut down, the cleaners were supposed to kill each other off."

"Right," Seven answered.

"Well, why bother trying to figure out who your target is? That wasn't part of the final mission. If he's really just some brainwashed killing machine, shouldn't his only focus be on killing Seven? Why worry about Vi? Why worry about completing whatever mission Seven might be on?"

"Sentry's reprogramming wasn't entirely successful on him," Seven said. "Reprogramming is supposed to eliminate emotion to make the cleaner more efficient at his job. Nikolai was sent back four times and he still feels…something. Based on these photos, he feels something for Vi and for whoever he thinks I'm going to kill. He's not the mindless killing machine they wanted him to be."

He's exactly like me.

Riddick pulled a disgusted face. "OK, so our guy is an attempted murderer, a kidnapper, and a stalker, but because he *means well* I shouldn't want to break every bone in his body? I'm calling bullshit on that."

"Damn straight," Lucas muttered.

Seven sighed. As nice as it was to see her brother and her mate agreeing on something, this wasn't the time or the situation she necessarily wanted their unity on. "I'm just saying he can be reasoned with. If we can convince him to let Vi go, and that I don't mean anyone any harm, maybe we can just all move on with our lives."

"No fucking way," Lucas grumbled at the same time Riddick said, "Fuck that shit."

Harper held up a placating hand. "Look, no one is saying we all have to hold hands and sing *Kumbaya* or anything. But Seven's right. If he's reasonable—which, I'm telling you he is—maybe we can get him to let Vi go and turn himself in to the Vampire Council for whatever punishment they feel is necessary."

"I don't know how you can call *this* dude," Lucas said, gesturing to the wall of surveillance photos, "*reasonable*."

"None of that matters anyway if we can't find the guy," Riddick added. "How about we worry about *where* he is before we worry about how to take him out?"

"You mean *down*," Harper corrected. "Take him *down*. Not take him *out*."

He shrugged. "Sure. We'll go with that for now."

Harper shot him a look that Seven had come to think of as her disapproving "mom" face. It was the same look Tina gave Harper and Marina whenever one of the girls made an inappropriate comment. She imagined Harper wouldn't appreciate the comparison, so Seven kept her mouth shut.

Seven's phone buzzed, startling her. "That's weird," she said. "The only people who ever call me are here." Reaching into her pocket, she checked the caller ID on the screen.

Violet Marchand calling.

Seven glanced up at Riddick. "Looks like the *where* problem is about to solve itself."

CHAPTER THIRTY-THREE

"Are you fucking insane?" Lucas hissed. "There's no way in *hell* I'm letting you do this."

It had been an hour since Nikolai had given Seven his location and told her to meet him. Seven hadn't laid out her plan until they reached the abandoned warehouse because she'd known Lucas wouldn't be happy. Neither would Riddick.

But she hadn't really counted on just how *much* they'd hate her plan.

Knowing there was no way she was going to sway Riddick, Seven decided to focus on Lucas. She grabbed his hands and laced her fingers through his. "Just give me a chance to talk to him before you and Riddick go in there to take him down. Maybe I can convince him to turn himself in."

His hands tightened on hers. "I can't take that chance. If something happens to you…"

He'd mourn her forever. That's what happened with wolves. They mated for life, and when a mated wolf died, the one left alive was never really the same again.

She tugged him closer so her body was pressed to his. "I have no intention of letting anything happen to me."

Lucas swallowed hard. "You're assuming he wants to talk at all. He might be planning to kill you as soon as you walk through the door."

Behind them, Harper cleared her throat. "He's not. He wants to talk to her. He wants to find out what mission she's carrying out. If he finds out that she was targeting someone dangerous, he plans to finish the mission after he kills her."

Lucas didn't take his eyes off Seven as he said, "Not helping, Harper."

Harper ignored him. "Just let us go in with you," she pleaded with Seven. "He didn't tell you to come alone. He must realize you'll bring someone with you."

"Cleaners always work alone," Seven told her. "He didn't tell me to come alone because it never occurred to him that I'd ever *ask* anyone to come with me."

"What about Benny?" Harper asked. "I can call him back. He can shift into his rat and sneak in with you. Nikolai would never know he's there."

"She's not going in there," Lucas practically roared. "I'm going."

"If anyone should go, it's me," Riddick argued. "This guy's a *dhampyre*, like me. You don't even know if you can take a *dhampyre* on your own."

Lucas bared his teeth at Riddick. "Try me."

Harper huffed out a disgusted noise. "Ugh. We get it. You're both big, strong, alpha men. Don't go whipping out your dicks and peeing on Seven just yet, alright? We'll figure something out."

"You guys are forgetting something," Seven began quietly. "I'm a *dhampyre*, too. I've had the same training Nikolai's had. I can take care of myself. Trust me." She pressed Lucas's hand to her heart. "*Please.*"

"Goddammit," he muttered, squeezing his eyes shut. "You're not going to let this go, are you?"

She shook her head. "He's like me, Lucas. Like I was, anyway. He's all alone. If I can convince him that another kind of life is possible, he has a chance to find what I have. Family. Friends. Love."

"You're not just trying to save Vi," Lucas said on an exhale, sounding like her words had drained all of his energy, leaving him feeling exhausted and defeated. "You want to save him, too."

"Like you saved me," she said, so quietly only he could hear her. "You could've given up on me and you never did. He deserves a chance."

He lowered his head so that their foreheads were touching. "I can't believe I'm actually considering this," he grumbled.

"I'm going to be fine," she assured him. "There's no one that can take me away from you. No one."

"Have you all lost your damn minds?" Riddick asked, voice thick with what-the-fuck. "He could kill her."

Lucas ignored him. "Are you absolutely sure about this?" he asked Seven.

"I am. I have to try."

He closed his eyes for a beat. "And you *promise* you'll get out of there if at any point it isn't working?"

She tightened her hands on his. "I promise."

"Twenty minutes," he said, his tone brooking no argument. "Not a second more. At twenty minutes, we're coming in, guns blazing."

"Twenty minutes," she agreed immediately. That was about nineteen more than she'd expected him to give her, so she considered it a huge victory. "Trust me."

With zero hesitation, he said, "I do."

The feeling threatening to choke her was so foreign it took a minute to identify it. Joy. Absolute, pure, unadulterated joy. This man who'd saved her and pieced the broken bits of her soul back together *trusted* her. He *loved* her. He was hers, and she was his.

Beyond words, she let go of one of his hands so that she could snake her hand around his neck and drag his mouth down to hers for a quick, hard kiss.

When they broke apart, Harper pressed her cell phone into Seven's hand. "There's a panic button on the home screen. Hit that if shit starts to go sideways. It rings to Riddick's phone. There's a tracer on there, too. Just in case."

"Wow," Seven said, "you guys are scarily prepared for situations like this."

Harper chuckled. "Not my first rodeo, sweetheart. If I had a dime for all the times I've been kidnapped…" she trailed off with a frown. "Well, I guess I'd have two dimes. I didn't really think that through. Not all that impressive or helpful, huh?"

Nope. Not at all. Seven patted her shoulder comfortingly anyway, and pocketed the cell phone. "It's fine. Don't worry. I've got this."

Harper tipped her head in Riddick's direction and said, "Don't tell me. Tell him."

Riddick was standing there, hands on hips, head tipped down, muscle in his cheek twitching under the force of his clenched jaw. In other words, he was the absolute picture of tense, fighting-for-self-control alpha male. He probably wouldn't appreciate it if she pointed out that his posture perfectly mirrored Lucas's at the moment.

Wordlessly, she wrapped her arms around his waist and rested her head against his chest. After a moment, he let out a harsh sigh and returned her hug.

Seven pulled back just far enough to look up at him. "I'll never be Grace, you know."

He frowned. "Sweetheart, I don't—"

"Grace was the person I would've been if our mom had lived," she interrupted. "If…Sentry hadn't existed. She'd probably be…an accountant or something. Someone's mom, maybe, living in the suburbs."

"That doesn't sound so bad," he mumbled.

"Grace would've been useless today." She smirked up at him. "I'm not useless. I'm going to go in there and I'm going to get him to surrender."

"And if he doesn't?"

"Then I'm going to kick his ass."

That earned her the smile she'd been hoping for. "You will, huh?"

"Absolutely. There's no way I can lose." She glanced back at Lucas. "I have way too much to live for these days."

CHAPTER THIRTY-FOUR

Violet's heart and stomach battled for a place in her throat as Seven walked into the warehouse, just as calm, cool, and collected as always. For once, she would've liked to see some concern on her patient's face. There was, after all, a highly trained assassin waiting for her. Was a little ninja-like vigilance too much to ask?

Seven lifted her chin in Vi's direction. "You good?" she asked.

Violet nodded. "I'm fine. But Seven, you need to get out of here. He's—"

"I know what he is and I know what he wants to do. It's fine. Don't worry."

Yeah, sure, no problem at all, right? Why worry about the six-foot-three, two-hundred-pound killer? Everything's just hunky-fuckin'-dory.

"754821," Nik said from behind her. "You're looking well."

Vi closed her eyes for a moment. It just wasn't *right* that he should have that voice. Lunatics should *sound* like lunatics. What was the world coming to when the bad guys sounded sexy?

Seven cocked her head to one side as she studied him. "I just go by Seven now. It's much less formal than 754821."

He chuckled and damned if the sound didn't shoot straight to Vi's lady bits. Stockholm syndrome, she thought. It was the only reasonable explanation for what she was feeling.

"You can call me Nikolai," he told Seven. "As you say, it's much less formal than 654590."

Vi's eyes bounced back and forth between them like she was watching a game of ping pong. And weren't they just the most polite people who were about to try and kill each other that she'd ever seen? It was all so surreal that she fought the urge to pinch herself. Maybe if she actually did, maybe she'd wake up and realize this had all been a terrible dream.

Vi gasped as Nikolai stepped around her and leveled a gun at Seven's chest. Seven didn't even bother to put her hands up. She just stared at Nikolai like she had exactly zero fucks to give. From where Vi was sitting—still *tied to the chair*—Seven's level of chill was badass and terrifying in equal measure.

"You don't have to do this, you know," Seven said.

His eyes narrowed on her. "Of course I do. We're the last. You know what needs to be done."

"I know that Sentry is gone and there's no reason for you to carry out their final orders."

We were supposed to die.

Vi couldn't hold back her squeak of alarm as she remembered Seven's words from the day they first met. If Sentry folded, the last cleaner was supposed to kill himself. It was like *Highlander*, only instead of gaining knowledge of all things, the one left standing got to commit *hari kari.*

Nikolai didn't just intend to kill Seven. He planned to kill himself, too!

Well…shit. That was a wholly unpleasant idea, Vi realized. Was it her Stockholm syndrome that made her heart hurt at the thought of Nikolai killing himself?

He let out a humorless chuckle. "You didn't see what became of the other cleaners without Sentry's guidance."

Seven nodded. "I heard. But you and I are different, aren't we, Nikolai? We've always been different. That's part of the reason you were sent for reprogramming so many times. Following their orders didn't come naturally to you. So why do it now?"

Nikolai's brow furrowed. "How do you know about that?"

Vi's stomach clenched at the thought of Nikolai enduring Sentry reprogramming four times. Many of her patients had been employed by Sentry at one time or another, and she'd seen pretty much all of the agency's policy and procedure books. Reprogramming for cleaners was really just a fancy term for torture, breaking the subjects down physically and emotionally until they doubted everything they were. When they were nearly incapable of trusting their own judgment, they were considered reprogrammed and usually followed orders without question from that point on.

"My sister-in-law is a psychic," Seven answered. "And my friends on the Council have your records."

This time, Nikolai's chuckle held the tiniest hint of genuine mirth. "Cleaners don't have families and friends. What angle are you playing? Who is your target?"

She shook her head. "I don't have a target."

"It's true," Vi blurted out. "And Riddick really is her brother. She's not lying."

Nikolai's jaw clenched, but Seven, oddly enough, smiled. "He knows that. He's like me. He can tell when someone's lying. Do you know about *dhampyres*, Nikolai?"

"Only rumors from the other cleaners," he murmured.

Rumors he was only now starting to understand he was a part of, Vi realized. She could see it on his face. He was struggling, but he was actually starting to believe Seven! He wasn't the inhuman monster Sentry had tried to turn him into. Which made her feel moderately better about her Stockholm syndrome. But only moderately.

"It's all true," Seven told him. "As far as I know, you and I were the only *dhampyre* cleaners. It's what made it possible for you to resist reprogramming so many times. Think about it, Nikolai. Sentry is gone. You know I don't have a target, so there's no reason to kill me. There's no reason to kill *yourself*. You can start over, just like I have."

He looked at her like she'd just sprouted a second head. "Just because you don't have a target…you think that makes you deserving of a life among regular, normal people?" He jerked his chin in Vi's direction. "You think you're fit to be with people like her? You think *I'm* fit to be with people like her?" The laugh he let out this time practically gave Vi frostbite. "We're killers, 754821. We. Don't. Deserve. To. Be. Here."

Seven let out a harsh breath. "I thought that way for a long time, too. But people like Vi helped me see I was wrong. We're not that different, Nikolai. I have friends and family now. I have *love*. And I get to spend the rest of my life with people I love while I do what I can to contribute to society. Maybe I don't deserve to be here right now." She shrugged. "But I won't stop trying to be worthy of what I've been given. And no one—not you, not *anyone*—will take that chance away from me."

And with that, Seven flung her hand out in Nikolai's direction. The gun flew out of his hand and sailed across the warehouse, smacking into the far wall before clattering to the ground.

There was a pregnant pause as Nikolai stared at the gun that Seven had managed to throw across the room without actually touching it. Then he said, "Nice parlor trick."

"Sorry," Seven said, sounding anything but. "I don't like guns being pointed at me. If you want to kill me, I'm afraid you're going to have to do it the hard way."

Vi swallowed hard. Was she crazy? Seven looked so tiny compared to Nikolai! And they'd had the exact same Sentry training. How did she think she could hold her own against him?

The smile Nikolai threw at Seven reminded Vi of a wolf baring its teeth at prey. "I'll tell you what, little one. You beat me in a *fair* fight? Maybe I'll believe you and turn myself over to the authorities. If you lose? We do things *my* way."

And by "his way", Vi could only assume he meant murder/suicide. This time she was pretty sure her gulp was audible. "Don't do this, Nikolai," she whispered.

He glanced her way and she gasped. The depth of emotion she saw in his eyes was staggering. Pity, remorse, regret, desire, longing…it was all right there. But then he blinked and it disappeared, making her wonder if it had all been a figment of her imagination. Or a result of her Stockholm syndrome.

"I'm sorry, *kotehok*," he murmured.

Seven tossed Vi her cell phone. "Press the panic button on the home screen if it looks like I'm about to lose. But not until then, OK?"

Vi nodded, fighting the urge to immediately press the panic button. Because what she was feeling right now? It was definitely *panic*. Throat-closing, heart-stopping, stomach-churning panic. She didn't want either one of them to lose!

Vi started gnawing on her thumbnail as they faced off. Their stances were so similar—knees bent ever so slightly, one leg further forward than the other, bodies turned diagonally, hands balled loosely near their faces—that Vi was once again reminded of how similar their training must have been. In instances where both fighters were equally skilled, didn't the bigger, stronger of the two always win?

But Seven wasn't about to just sit around and let herself get beat. Apparently, her speed leveled the playing field between them a bit. Before Vi could even blink, Seven shot forward, whipped her leg behind Nikolai's, and dumped him on his ass.

But Nikolai wasn't exactly slow either, and before she could strike again, he'd leapt to his feet in a smooth, fluid motion that up until then, Vi had only ever seen Bruce Lee accomplish.

"I underestimated you," Nikolai said.

Seven smirked at him. "Most people do."

Seven managed to evade his next two strikes and block a third, but Nikolai caught her wrist and threw her to the concrete in a move that must have wrenched her shoulder something awful. He moved to kick her while she was down, but Seven rolled and kicked out at the same time, catching his upper inner thigh. He went down.

They both stood up slowly this time, eyeing each other more cautiously than before. Maybe Seven had underestimated Nikolai as well?

What happened next had Vi's finger twitching over the panic button. They clashed in a blur almost too fast for her human eyes to track, going at each other with everything they had in a brutal mix of martial arts, grappling, and brute force. He punched, she blocked. She kicked, he ducked. On and on it went. It was almost graceful in its brutal precision, like a kind of violent ballet.

Nikolai caught her next punch, spun her around, and manhandled her into what looked to be a bone-crunching bear hug. She clawed at his arm, but even Vi could see the veins and tendons popping out under his skin as he tightened his hold.

Vi pointed to the panic button. "Now?"

Seven's face was turning red, but she still managed to force a surprisingly firm "No" past her bloodless lips.

Vi was about to argue when Seven threw her leg up in a move that would make any Rockette proud, somehow managing to kick high enough to catch Nikolai in the face.

So, apparently, speed wasn't Seven's only advantage over Nikolai. She also had Gumby-like flexibility. Huh. Maybe it was a fair fight after all.

Nikolai dropped her and swiped a hand under his bleeding nose. A nose that now listed slightly to the left, obviously broken from Seven's kick.

Not that it slowed him down any. He dodged the hard left hook Seven threw at him, and managed to catch her with a glancing blow to her temple. Vi sucked in a sharp breath, sure that a hit like that must hurt like a bitch, but Seven just shook it off.

Nikolai threw a kick at Seven's head, but she ducked under it, moving into a leg sweep, knocking Nikolai onto his back. She was on him before he could leap up. Seven tried to punch him, but he caught her fist.

They froze like that, muscles tensed. Seven bared her teeth at him, obviously struggling against his superior strength.

He smirked up at her. "You're good, but you'll never be stronger than me."

"You're right about that," she said through clenched teeth. "But I have one giant advantage at the moment."

"What's that?"

"I don't have balls."

And with that, she shifted and kneed him in the balls so hard that even Vi winced. Good thing he'd turned out to be the bad guy. If she'd wanted to ever have kids with him, she wasn't sure that was any longer an option.

His face went completely white, but save a pained grunt, he made no other noise. Vi imagined most men would be in tears. But Nikolai worked through the pain, managing to arch his back with enough force to throw Seven off him. Not only that, but in a wrestling move that all but defied physics, he was somehow able to reverse their positions.

She bucked and tried to throw a punch, but he grabbed her arm and wrenched with enough force that Vi was pretty sure she heard Seven's shoulder joint pop out of its socket.

Much like Nikolai, Seven didn't cry out or give up like a normal person would. Pain was clearly etched on her face, but with what could only be called a battle cry, she arched up and threw him off her.

They both climbed unsteadily to their feet, her cradling her arm against her stomach, him wiping blood from his nose and hunching over (with his balls probably lodged somewhere up near his spleen, if Vi imagined correctly), looking like they'd fought a years-long war.

Seven was the first to move. She straightened her spine, lifted her chin, and gave him a come-and-get-it gesture with her good arm. She could go another twelve rounds, her defiant expression screamed.

His jaw dropped in surprise for a split second, but just as quickly, his eyes narrowed, and with a growl, he prowled toward her again.

And that's when everything went a little…sideways.

CHAPTER THIRTY-FIVE

The noise level was damn-near deafening as Riddick, Harper, and a fully shifted Lucas stormed the warehouse. Seven wasn't sure if it was Lucas or Riddick who broke the door down, but there was now so little of it that it looked like it'd been through a wood chipper.

Before she could say a word, Nikolai was flat on his back with the wolf's teeth at his throat. Vi found her voice first. "No!" she shrieked. "Don't hurt him!"

Riddick snorted as he cut the ties at Vi's ankles. "No worries, doc. Looks like he'll be out of his misery soon enough. It'll be so fast it probably won't even hurt. Much."

Harper rolled her eyes. "Real sensitive, hon. Seven, sweetie, if you could let Lucas know you're alright, you might be able to convince him to, uh, you know, not rip out the dude's throat. That'd be great. I had a big breakfast and I'd rather not see it again, if you know what I mean."

Seven's adrenaline rush from the fight was dying down, and she had to shake off her growing lethargy as she dropped to her knees at Nikolai's side. "Lucas," she whispered. "Please don't kill him. Violet is fine. I'm fine."

The wolf snarled and tightened his hold on Nikolai's throat. Nikolai didn't move a muscle, other than to shift his gaze to Vi, who was fidgeting nervously, looking absolutely terrified.

Seven let out a frustrated sigh. "Why did you hit the panic button, Vi? I had it under control."

"I didn't!" Vi sputtered. "And I'd say that 'under control' is a matter of opinion. You two were beating the shit out of each other! I wasn't sure either one of you would stop!"

"Lucas heard you scream, Seven," Harper said. "He shifted and ran for the door before we even knew what the hell was going on."

Ugh. This was her own damn fault then, Seven realized. She leaned forward and buried her hand in the wolf's thick fur, then rested her forehead against his side. "Don't kill him, Lucas. Let the Council take him. He was confused and made a mistake. He doesn't deserve to die for it any more than I deserve to die for the mistakes I made. Just shift back now. Please, Lucas. For me."

The wolf let out one last angry snort before releasing its grip on Nikolai's throat. The entire room sighed in relief. And a moment later, Lucas shifted back and threw his arms around Seven, taking care not to jostle her dislocated shoulder. She buried her nose in the crook of his neck and breathed his familiar scent deep into her lungs.

"I don't know what I would've done if something had happened to you," he murmured.

She snuggled in closer. "I told you I'd be fine. Too much to live for, remember?"

"Don't *ever* ask me to let you put yourself in that kind of danger *ever* again."

"I won't. I promise. I love you, Lucas."

"I love you, too. So much."

"Oh, for God's sake," Riddick grumbled. "Put on some damn pants."

And with that, a pair of black sweat pants smacked Lucas in the face. He stood up, lifting Seven with him, and put on the pants, which Harper had apparently stuffed in her oversized handbag before they drove to the warehouse. "You just never know," she said.

Nikolai stood up, and Harper promptly pulled her Ruger out and pointed it at his head. "No sudden moves, pal. Just because we aren't going to kill you doesn't mean I'm entirely opposed to putting a couple bullets in you."

Riddick grumbled his sincere agreement, but Nikolai just looked up at her, slightly confused. "You…you all came here for…her?"

"That's what family does, asshat," Harper spat back without hesitation.

His brow furrowed like he was unfamiliar with the word. "Family," he murmured. He shifted his gaze to Lucas, then back to Seven. "And love. It *is* true, isn't it?"

He sounded so amazed that Seven felt a stab of empathy for him. He probably hadn't known the kind of love and support she'd found since his parents were taken from him. Nikolai was basically *her* before Lucas and Harper and Riddick found her.

Great. Now she had a lump of emotion in her throat that felt like it a chunk of burning coal. "It's true. All of it. I know I didn't technically win that fight, but if you agree to turn yourself in anyway,

I'll put in a good word for you with the Council. You can start a real life."

Lucas gripped her tighter and Riddick opened his mouth—no doubt to object—but slammed it shut again when Harper not-so-discreetly stomped on his foot.

Nikolai shook his head and ran a shaking hand through his disheveled hair. "You did win the fight, little one. I couldn't have gone on much longer. You simply…wanted it more." He shrugged. "Now I understand why."

Because she had more to live for than he did, Seven realized.

"You can have it all too, you know," she told him. "You can't bring your family back, but you can create a new one."

Seven didn't miss that his gaze shifted ever-so-slightly to Vi for a split second before meeting hers again. He chuckled. "I doubt that's in the cards for me. But…I'm willing to turn myself over to the Council." He jerked his chin in Harper's direction. "You can put your weapon away. I'll go willingly."

"Oh, I wasn't *really* going to shoot you," Harper said, tucking the gun away in her purse. But if Riddick thought I might, I figured it would keep him from breaking your legs or ripping your arms off or anything."

"Um…thank you?"

"Yeah, sure. No prob."

Riddick frowned at her. "Is that the only reason you ever draw your gun?"

"No, of course not, hon." Then, to Vi, she nodded and mouthed, "It totally is."

Nikolai reached for Seven's hand. "May I help with that shoulder?"

She wasn't looking forward to it, but Seven knew she didn't really have any other options if she wanted to be able to move her arm again. She knew Lucas and Riddick wouldn't want to hurt her, and she damn sure wasn't going to the hospital. Nikolai was her best chance.

"Alright," she said, bracing back against Lucas as Nikolai lifted her arm. "But do it qui—"

Seven's vision blurred and she was forced to swallow a pained cry as Nikolai tugged on her arm, then shoved the joint back in place. "Thank you," she choked out.

His answering smirk made her want to smack him around some more. She gestured to his nose. "Can *I* help *you* with that?"

The smirk died on his lips, but he nodded manfully.

She smiled sweetly up at him as she placed her hands on either side of his nose. She waited until he started to ask what she was waiting for before she snapped it back in place.

The barest whisper of a pained grunt escaped his lips before he glared down at her and muttered, "*Спасибо.*"

Her smile grew. "You're welcome."

After a moment, he grudgingly returned her smile.

"What the fuck is this all about?" Riddick grumbled.

"This must be how cleaners make up," Harper stage-whispered. "It's kind of sweet…in a weirdly violent kind of way."

Hunter and Mischa arrived about twenty minutes later. Hunter whisked Nikolai away to Council headquarters, and Mischa took Vi home.

Riddick drove Harper, Lucas, and Seven back to the Harper Hall Investigations building, where Lucas had left his car. In the parking lot, when Riddick and Harper turned to go inside, Lucas said, "Wait. I need you to hear this."

Taking Seven's hands, he said, "By shifter law, we're already married. But here's the thing. I was going to ask you to marry me the old-fashioned human way, too. Maybe sometime this summer or fall. But I changed my mind."

Even though she saw him trying not to smile, there was a tiny little part of Seven that braced at his words and berated herself for believing—even for a moment—in happy endings for someone like her.

"After what happened today," he said. "I don't want to wait until summer or fall to marry you. I want to marry you *now*."

She blinked at him. "Now?"

"Well, not tonight, obviously. But as soon as we can arrange it. Everything that happened tonight…" he paused, as if chilled by the memory. "It made me realize I don't ever want to be without you again. If you want me, I intend to ask your brother for your hand in marriage. And then you better get used to having me around, because I'm not going anywhere."

Seven felt as if all the air had just been sucked out of her lungs. "*If* I want you?" she asked, stunned. "Are you crazy? I've wanted you since the beginning!"

Then he kissed her in a way he never had before, slow and reverent. His right hand curled around the nape of her neck, and the other stroked her now-wet cheeks.

"Don't cry," he murmured. "I can't take it."

"I'm not crying," she answered. She totally was, though. "I never thought I'd have this. You. Us. I've never felt this before. I'm so…happy."

"It's new for me too, beautiful," he said, brushing the hair off her forehead. "But there's no one else for me. If you give me the chance, I'll spend the rest of my life making sure you stay happy."

"Yes," she whispered.

"Ugh, I'm gonna puke," Riddick muttered, holding his stomach and looking a little green, like he really might vomit at any minute.

With a sigh, Lucas let go of Seven and held his hand out to Riddick. "I know we haven't always gotten along. But I love your sister and I want—no, I *need*—to spend the rest of my life with her. I know I don't deserve her, but no one will ever love her more or try harder to make her happy than I will. Do we have your permission?"

Riddick stared at his hand for a minute with an ugly scowl riding his features. But when Harper jabbed her elbow into his ribs, he sighed and took it. "Yes, damn it. You have my permission."

Then he let go of Lucas's hand and punched him in the stomach with a quick jab.

Lucas grunted, but didn't double over. "What the fuck was that for?" he growled.

"That's for touching my sister in the first place," Riddick growled right back.

"I'm marrying her, for Christ's sake!"

"That's why you're not dead."

"Um…thanks?"

He sniffed and looked away. "You're welcome. Whatever."

"Aw, this is so beautiful!" Harper cried, then pulled them all in tight. "Group hug!"

In the middle of that group hug, Seven realized that she'd managed to find something more precious than she ever could've imagined. These people were more than just family. No matter where she went or what happened or what she did, these people would always be there for her. They were her true north. They were *home.*

She'd told Riddick she could never be Grace, and that was true. But what Seven hadn't realized until this very moment, was that she owed everything she had to Grace Riddick. Grace had died so that Seven could live. And by God, Seven intended to live and love enough for both of them. Grace's sacrifice would *not* be in vain.

"Thank you, Grace," she whispered. "I owe you one."

The End

(But stay tuned for Violet's story, coming November, 2017!)

A personal note from Isabel:

If you enjoyed this book, first of all, thanks! It would mean a lot to me if you would take a moment and show your support of indie authors (like me) by leaving a review on Amazon or Goodreads. Your reviews are a very important part of helping readers discover new books.

Want to know more about me, or when the next book release is? You can email me directly at: isabel.jordan@izzyjo.com. Also feel free to stalk me on:

BookBub: https://www.bookbub.com/authors/isabel-jordan

Facebook: https://www.facebook.com/SemiCharmedAuthor

Twitter:@izzyjord

Pinterest: https://www.pinterest.com/ijordan0345/

Goodreads: https://www.goodreads.com/author/show/8523573.Isabel_Jordan

Website: http://www.izzyjo.com/

Thanks so much, and happy reading!

Sincerely,

Isabel

About the author

The normal:

Isabel Jordan writes because it's the only profession that allows her to express her natural sarcasm and not be fired. She is a paranormal and contemporary romance author. Isabel lives in the U.S. with her husband, ten-year-old son, a senile beagle, a neurotic shepherd mix, and a ginormous Great Dane mix.

The weird:

Now that the normal stuff is out of the way, here's some weird-but-true facts that would never come up in polite conversation. Isabel Jordan:

1. Is terrified of butterflies (don't judge...it's a real phobia called lepidopterophobia)

2. Is a lover of all things ironic (hence the butterfly on the cover of *Semi-Charmed*)

3. Is obsessed with *Supernatural*, *Game of Thrones*, *The Walking Dead*, and *Dog Whisperer.*

4. Hates coffee. Drinks a Diet Mountain Dew every morning.

5. Will argue to the death that *Pretty in Pink* ended all wrong. (Seriously, she ends up with the guy who was embarrassed to be seen with her and not the nice guy who loved her all along? That would never fly in the world of romance novels.)
6. Would eat Mexican food every day if given the choice.

7. Reads two books a week in varied genres.

8. Refers to her Kindle as "the precious."

9. Thinks puppy breath is one of the best smells in the world.

10. Is a social media idgit. (Her husband had to explain to her what the point of Twitter was. She's still a little fuzzy on what Instagram and Pinterest do.)

11. Kicks ass at Six Degrees of Kevin Bacon.

12. Stole her tagline idea ("weird and proud") from her son. Her tagline idea was, "Never wrong, not quite right." She liked her son's idea better.

13. Breaks one vacuum cleaner a year because she ignores standard maintenance procedures (Really, you're supposed to empty the canister every time you vacuum? Does that seem excessive to anyone else?)

14. Is still mad at the WB network for cancelling *Angel* in 2004.

15. Can't find her way from her bed to her bathroom without her glasses, but refused eye surgery, even when someone else offered to pay. (They lost her at "eye flap". Seriously, look it up. Scary stuff.)

Made in the USA
Columbia, SC
21 November 2020

25119724R00148